Thirty Seconds To Life

Based on a True Story

Kitty Kaye

Front cover illustrated by
Debbe Femiak

*This story is
dedicated to Jacob Miller.
Although he is not a real person,
his story is hauntingly
similar with one that is.*

FOREWORD

Although this story is based on actual events, some of it has been fictionalized for fundamental reasons. Yes, some of these events actually happened, as sad as it may be. However, the reason for telling this story is not to point fingers or cause any ill feelings for what might have been an oversight in life. It is simply to show what can happen if you let the challenges of life get away from you or fail to guard your steps in life carefully.

I believe life is meant to be gratifying and enjoyable to all. Oh, sure, there are plenty of trials and heartaches along the way. Yet, we need to allow ourselves to learn from the words written within the pages of this book. It's important to make good choices and not let life take you down the path of no return. Learning from someone else's mistakes can keep you from becoming stranded in the same boat – or in a jail cell, as is the case in this story.

Always try to live life well. Walk carefully, be cautious, keep your eyes open, your mind clear, and your life on track. You will never regret making good decisions, which will ultimately result in a fulfilling life for yourself and those around you. A few brief seconds of poor decision-making can alter the course of your life forever. That's all it took in this case – just a thirty-second mistake that lasted for a lifetime of heartache.

TABLE OF CONTENTS

CHAPTER 1
The Beginning of the End

"Jacob!" I heard someone calling my name, but the voice seemed faint, incredibly small, and extremely far away. It was almost as though it was coming through an elongated tunnel, from somewhere out beyond the realms of earth. For a moment, I was tempted to look up, expecting to see an angel or God Himself calling to me.

"Jacob! Jacob Paul! Listen to me!"

They were using my middle name. The only time anyone used my middle name was when I was in very serious trouble. Had I done something wrong?

"Give me the gun, Jake!" the voice insisted.

A gun? I had a gun? What was I doing with a gun? I looked down at my hand, and almost jumped in astonishment. The voice was right! There was a gun in my hand! How did it get there? And even worse than that, what had I just done with it?

I slowly turned toward the voice and tried to focus on the face that housed it. I knew it was a familiar voice, but everything was a blur. It was almost as though I was watching a scary movie with a projector that was out of focus. It was a movie in which I didn't really want to know what had happened, yet wanted to know the ending at the same time. Like the time I had watched the original Jurassic Park movie as a child, with a blanket over my head, peaking through a hole. It was too scary to face, yet I was too curious to not know.

I glanced down at my hand again and realized the gun was still there. This time I realized there was also another hand there, a much smaller hand, trying to take the gun away from me. Apparently, I had been resisting this hand and not allowing it to gain control. Still, I didn't know why.

Who did this hand belong to? It was as familiar as the voice, but I couldn't seem to place either of them. Was this some kind of bad dream?

Why couldn't I see clearly? I had no idea where I was, what had just happened, or who this person was that wanted my gun. Yet, one thing was clear. Something terribly wrong had just occurred, something so life altering and drastic that my mind didn't seem to want to process it. As hard as I tried, I just couldn't make my brain form any connections or bring any logic to the scene before me.

One thing I knew I had to do, though. I had to let go of the gun. Whatever was happening, I knew possessing a gun could only make it worse. I slowly relaxed my grip on the gun, and the smaller hand quickly took it away. I watched the gun escape from the grasp of my hand, almost as if it was in slow motion. I kept an eye on the gun as the distance between my hand and the gun grew, and allowed my gaze to travel up the arm from the smaller hand to the face of the body it belonged to.

Almost as if someone turned the light on in the midst of the darkest room, I realized who the little hand belonged to. It was my wife. She was the one who had been calling my name. But what kind of chaotic disaster were we currently caught up in? She seemed to understand better than I did, knowing that the priority at the moment was gaining control of the gun.

Feeling as though a little rationalization was coming back to me, I began to look around our setting. People had started to gather around us, glancing briefly our way, and their expressions told a story of horror, of unbelief, of shock. Some people looked past us toward the cars parked on the side of the road. Almost as if still looking through fog or the haze of a hot summer day, I followed their gaze. What I saw made my face reflect the horror of those standing nearby. There was a body lying in the road beside one of the cars, face down, with streams of blood flowing out from beneath her.

Suddenly, my brain made a connection and I turned sharply toward my wife. I had been holding a gun! And now there was a body lying in the road! Had I caused that to happen? Had I been the reason for the demise of that soul? What on earth had I just done?

I was able to zone in on my wife's face, and it told me all I needed to know. Her expression reflected the same horror as those around us. I needed to know what I had done, but before I had a chance to ask any questions, I heard a voice of authority calling over the buzz in my brain.

"Police!" the voice called out. "I'm a police officer. Put your hands in the air where I can see them!"

I looked in the direction of the voice, but I didn't see any police officer. Instead, I saw a man in shorts and a T-shirt running toward me, and he looked like he meant business. He was clearly not interested in anything but putting me out of commission. He was charging directly at me, as if I was the only person on the planet, and his main goal was to take me down.

My natural instinct was to run. I still wasn't fully aware of what was happening, what I had done, or why this man seemingly wanted to kill me. Yet, the one thing I did know was that I didn't belong in this situation. I was a good person, who had never been in serious trouble before, and I didn't want to be now. I just wanted to get away from this bad dream and wake up in a better place.

The fear factor kicked in, and I promptly turned around and ran. It was a part of my nature. I had never been an aggressive person. When trouble came my way, I had always avoided it like the plague. I ran from adversity, and usually went well out of my way to avoid it. But avoiding it didn't seem to be an option at this moment. The adversary was tight on my tail, and apparently in much better shape than I was. My days of inactivity due to unemployment from my physical illness had left my body a bit neglected. I clearly did not have the capacity to outrun this person, whoever he might be, and for whatever reason he might be pursuing me. It seemed the appropriate thing to do was to stop and face up to whatever evil deed I might have just committed.

I ran far enough to get away from the view of the crowd, around a corner and out of sight. Then I stopped and turned to face the approaching fitness guru. My goal was to ask him what had happened and what crime I had committed, but he wasn't interested in talking. He charged at me like a Navy seal, whose instructions were to maim, kill, or destroy, whichever seemed the most appropriate at the moment.

His charge knocked me off balance and I landed on the ground. He quickly put his knee in the middle of my back and pulled my hands behind me. It seemed he must be a police officer, as he was clearly trained to overtake and quickly gain control of a situation. I might have had more body mass, but he was muscular, skilled, and in good physical shape. I was no competition for his ability, not that I was ready to resist anyway. I knew something was wrong, and still hoped this was the nightmare of all night-mares. I would have given anything to wake up in a cold sweat and realize that it hadn't really happened.

However, within moments, I heard sirens coming. Lots of sirens. Enough sirens to make me realize that this was not a dream. It sounded like every police car within the town limits was headed our way, and I think it was all because of me. The weight on my back and the pressure holding my arms firmly behind me told me that I would be their main focus.

Why wouldn't my brain clear so I could remember what had happened? Maybe it was a form of protection. My brain didn't want me to know. It knew I wasn't ready to accept it, like when something tragic happens and your mind needs time to process it all. You have to go through stages to reason it all out, and my brain wasn't ready to do that. This must have been more than my stressed out brain could handle.

All too soon, the sirens pulled up nearby and stopped.

"He's over here," the man on my back called out.

Several officers rushed over to help him. One offered a pair of handcuffs, and I soon found myself in a state of restraint. I didn't know at the time, but my life of free choice had just ended. Although the handcuffs were temporary, I had tasted my last bite of freedom. I would never know independence again.

"Stand him up and bring him over here," one man instructed, possibly the police chief. With so many men in uniforms surrounding me, it was hard to tell who was who.

A couple of officers helped me to my feet, but not as a kind gesture. They were treating me roughly, and it didn't take long to realize that they all despised me. They were clearly mad at me for whatever I had done. They pushed and shoved me back around the corner to where the crowd had grown larger, and led me over beside one of the police cars. But they didn't put me into the car. They forced me to sit on the sidewalk, hands still cuffed behind me, while they began to investigate the scene and determine what to do next.

I wasn't accustomed to being treated so roughly. They were acting like I was the worse criminal alive. However, as I sat on the sidewalk and observed, I began to process the scene and realized maybe I did rank at the top of the list of evil outlaws. Many of the spectators were crying, weeping openly at the appalling scene. My gaze kept wandering over to the body in the road, which they had now covered with a sheet, out of respect for the deceased. Who was she? And how did her life end so abruptly in such a hideous manner, on a quiet street in what was typically a peaceful town?

Who knows how long I sat on the cold, hard sidewalk. One officer stood guard over me, almost as though he expected me to run again. The other officers were all quite occupied working the scene. The time on the ground gave me the opportunity to try to clear my brain. Glimpses started coming back.

I could hear my wife's voice yelling at me. I had obviously done something that greatly upset her, and she wasn't afraid to let me know she was not happy. I remembered driving down the road, feeling like my life was out of control, that I didn't want to exist anymore. Then there was a stranger confronting me, charging at me like she wanted to kill me, just like the fitness guru in the gym shorts. Why was everyone so upset with me? What had I done to anger so many people? As hard as I tried, I still couldn't make any sensible connections.

A short time later, a couple of officers returned and focused their attention on me. They each wore hate on their face, and I could tell I was the source of their rage.

"Let's get him up and take him to the station," one of them suggested. They once again stood me up, and none too gently either. As they led me to the closest police car, I turned to ask them what I had done. But they clearly weren't interested in talking to me. They just forced me into the car, driving my head into the top of the door frame in the process of it all.

"Ouch!" I cried out in pain, but there was no sympathy to be had. I probably deserved that, I reasoned to myself, as I climbed into the car. It would have been nice to be able to rub my aching head, but the handcuffs prevented that. All I could do was sit in the back of the car and try not to think about the throbbing pain.

They brought me down to the police station and threw me into an empty cell. As the metal door clanged shut behind me, fear gripped my heart. I was incarcerated! I had never even been inside a jail before, and now here I was behind the wrong side of the bars.

The officers all walked away and left me there. I had never felt so alone in my entire life. To say I was scared was definitely an understatement. I was petrified, terrified beyond words, paralyzed with fear. And, quite frankly, I wished I would die. Whatever was happening in my life, it wasn't anything I wanted to be a part of. I wanted out of this prison cell, and out of this dilemma. I would have given anything to be able to run away and flee to a new life, but it was apparent that I would not be going anywhere any time soon.

My frozen brain slowly began to thaw sitting in that bleak, barren jail cell, and I longed to be held by someone who loved me. I wanted my wife, my mom, my dad, or even my sister, Kelli – someone who would rub my back and reassure me that everything would be okay. Yet, I knew it wasn't okay, and that it might never be again.

As I sat on the edge of the bed, I slowly started to rock back and forth. And then the tears began to flow. What had I done? What could possibly have gone wrong? It was something I repeatedly asked myself over and over.

"What have you done, Jacob?" I sobbed out loud to myself. "What on earth have you done?"

I cried like I had never cried before. I sobbed until my whole body shook and my stomach hurt.

"What did you do, Jacob?" I demanded of myself. "How could you have gotten yourself into a situation like this? What has gone wrong with your life? How did it come to this?"

The tears flowed freely. I couldn't have stopped them if I wanted to. I wanted to apologize, to tell everyone I was sorry, that it was all a mistake and I hadn't meant any harm. Yet, I knew it was too late. Nothing I could say or do could fix the damage that had already been done.

I continued to rock back and forth on that uncomfortable bed, sobbing until my strength was gone. Finally, after what seemed like just short of forever, a man in a suit came to my cell and asked if I would like to talk. He needed to take my statement.

My statement? That meant he wanted to know my version of what had happened tonight. But could I explain it in a way that made sense? I wasn't sure I understood it all myself. Yet, I had to defend myself, make him understand that I wasn't a bad person who went around seeking to harm others. I had been a law abiding citizen all of my life, even though life hadn't always been fair to me.

In fact, my problems had started long ago, but I would have plenty of time to reason that all out later. Right now, I had to focus on the events of tonight. I didn't realize it at the time, but I would have many hours sitting behind bars to figure out exactly what had gone wrong in my life that led me to this horrific night. This night had proven to be the beginning of the end of my life.

CHAPTER 2
A Second Chance

"Jacob, did you hear me?" the voice was asking. It was a familiar voice, but my brain had stopped processing after her last words. I turned to look at my mother, trying hard to hold back the tears.

She rubbed my back and said, "I'm sorry, honey, but it's just not going to work. Your father and I tried, but we are not meant to be together. You will still have plenty of time with both of us, though. We will be fair and share joint custody."

Joint custody, my mind wailed. Whatever "joint custody" was, I didn't want it. I wanted my family – my mom, my dad and my sister, Kelli – just the way we had always been. The four of us had been the perfect family, or so I had thought.

I had been born the second child of Thomas and Brenda Miller. My sister was three years older than me, but had always seemed so much more mature than I was. My parents were career-minded, and both held successful jobs. We had established a good life for ourselves. My dad had built our house and we lived on a rural road with very little traffic. Hushed Hollow Road had been the perfect place to build a house, and it had a big yard for my sister and me to play in. What more did we need?

I had always thought our situation was ideal. Added to the perfection of our lives was the fact that my father's parents lived just down the road, easily within walking distance from our home. Since they were both retired, we could go visit Grammy and Grampy Miller any time. Their home was always open, and they eagerly welcomed us whenever we stopped by. Why couldn't my mother be happy with the way we were?

"You can stay with your father for now, just until I can get a place of my own," my mother explained. She was clearly set on leaving. "Once I am settled, we will work out the visitation schedule. It will be okay, Jakie. I promise."

I didn't want a visitation schedule. I didn't want her to be "settled" somewhere else. I wanted her to stay with us. I wanted a home, complete with an entire family, including both my mother and my father. But how could a five-year-old boy make his parents decide to stay together? Maybe I was the reason they were separating. Maybe I had done something wrong.

So I asked, "Is it my fault, Mom? Did I do something to make you want to leave?"

But my mother was reassuring. It wasn't me. Mom insisted that I hadn't said or done anything wrong. She just wasn't happy and couldn't live like this anymore. She had to go, and so she did.

For nights, I cried myself to sleep. I missed my mother. My dad did what he could to try to fill the gap, but he wasn't mom. A boy needs his mother, someone to tuck him in at night, read him a bedtime story, and kiss him on the forehead. My father would tuck me in, but he lacked the tender touch that a mother has. Every night after he shut off the light and closed my bedroom door, I would pull the blankets over my head and sob myself quietly to sleep. Without my mother, there was a big hole in my heart.

Oh, sure, I visited her on the weekends. But life as I had known it for the last five years was over. I knew for the rest of my childhood, I would drift back and forth between dad's house and mom's. Would either of them ever feel like home?

If my sister was as troubled with the change as I was, she didn't show it. She seemed content to be able to talk to mom on the phone, even if she couldn't be with her. She adjusted to our mother's departure much better than I did.

Maybe it was her mothering skills that kicked in and kept her going. She helped dad with dinner and the housework, and spent plenty of time doting on me. Being three years older than me, she had always adored me. But now she worked hard at trying to fill the gap left by mom's absence.

"Come on, Jakie," she would call up the stairs almost every weekday morning. "The bus will be here soon. If you don't hurry, we are going to miss it."

It didn't really matter to me if we missed it. I was too busy playing with Matchbox cars in my bedroom. Plus, what five-year-old boy wants to go to school and sit at a desk all day anyway? I could find better things to do with my time.

But when I heard those heavy footsteps coming up the stairs, I jumped up and grabbed my backpack. They were much too heavy for my sister, and it could only mean one thing – dad was coming for me. I certainly didn't want to start the day with the wrath of dad to deal with.

When it was time to head out to the bus, he expected me to go – no questions asked, and I knew better than to argue.

****

Who knows how long it took for the adjustment period, but one day I realized I was no longer sad and blue. Dividing my time between homes became part of my normal routine. Mom had settled close by in a fairly new housing development named Evergreen Heights, just a few minutes away from dad's place. It became easy to commute back and forth between the two homes.

Then one day, an amazing thing happened. My mom remarried, and I instantly had brothers. We were kind of like the Brady Bunch, with an instant six kids. He had four, and my mother had two. He brought two boys and two girls into the union – Mason, Jacob, Mariah and Alicia, so it amounted to three boys and three girls, just like the Brady family.

I couldn't have been happier. I had always wanted a brother to play with, and now I had two. My new brothers were older than me, but I was fine with that. Plus, it was comical how one of them had the same name as me! What are the chances of that happening?!

The two of us who bore the same name became known as Big Jake and Little Jake. For awhile, everyone tried calling the older one Jacob and me Jake, but that was too confusing. We would both automatically answer. It seemed that Big Jake and Little Jake just worked better. No child likes to be thought of as "little," but I had always wanted to have an older brother, so I was okay with it.

Then one day I realized that my middle name was Paul, just like my stepfather's name. So, I asked my mom if I could be called Jakie, Jr.

"Well, you're not really a 'junior,' honey," she patiently explained. "When you are a 'junior,' it means you have the same exact name as your father – first, middle, and last name. The only name you have in common with Paul is your middle name."

"That's okay," I insisted. "You can still call my Jakie, Jr. can't you? I am the second Jake in the family now, since Big Jake is older than me."
My mom just smiled and agreed that I did seem like a "Jakie, Jr." She didn't see any reason why they couldn't call me that. So, that became my new nickname, quickly adopted and accepted by the rest of the family.

I adored my older siblings. I now had some role models, and we all seemed to get along just fine, for the most part. In fact, at times we got along too well. We could become foolish during our times together, and sometimes get a little carried away. Like the time my mother was making spaghetti for dinner. She left the girls in charge of the spaghetti as it cooked, while she went to take a shower. However, the girls got busy with girl talk, so the boys took over, and you know how boys can take over!

When my mother came out of the bathroom, she found our dinner firmly mounted on the dining room wall. We had had a spaghetti fight while she was occupied in the bathroom. It had been a lot of fun, but she did not see the humor in it. Not at all! I can't remember ever seeing my mother any madder than she was that night. We quickly learned to curb our appetite for adventure. Throwing spaghetti across the dining room was clearly not on the list of ways to succeed in life.

My new stepfather, Paul Rapini, proved to be a family-oriented man, and for several years, life was good. In fact, it wasn't just good, it was great. It seemed I had been given a second chance at childhood.

Summer time, naturally, was our favorite time of the year. We lived close to Crystal Lake, and every weekend we spent with mom found us at its shoreline. We would pack a picnic lunch, or bring some meat for grilling and head to Sandy Beach to have a barbeque. My mom would make some salads (usually macaroni and potato), pack some chips, an assortment of soda, a watermelon, and we would have a summer time feast. It was great to be alive, enjoying time together with my family, overlooking the beautiful lake, and eating delicious food.

I learned to swim in the lake that first summer. We all loved the water, adults and kids included. My new sisters were both younger than me, but they loved the water, too. Paul would pick the three of us up, one at a time, and launch us into the water. We loved it! It briefly felt like we could fly, before crashing down into the cool, refreshing water. It just didn't seem like life could get any better.

However, it did. My mom was soon pregnant, and not just once, but twice. She gave us a little brother, named Ricky, and a couple years later blessed us with a sweet little baby sister, whom she named Nicole. I didn't realize at the time how close Ricky and I would become. I fell in love with him the minute I saw him, and the affection was returned. Even as a baby, he would crawl over any barrier to get to me. When he learned to walk, he followed me around like I was all that mattered in life. We were two peas in a pod. The age difference didn't really seem to matter, except when I wanted to hang out with my friends. Sometimes, it was hard to sneak away when Little Ricky was always tagging along behind.

Most of the time, I didn't mind it, though. When he got older, I helped him learn to ride his bike. Then we would ride our bikes around the housing development after school and on weekends, or occasionally we would play catch in the yard. It got so sometimes my weekends at dad's house were lonely. When I was at my mother's house, there was always someone to hang out with and something to do. When I went to dad's, it was just the three of us. Dad always seemed busy, working on the garden or the house, and Kelli was into girl stuff. Playing ball in the yard just wasn't her thing. It was like I lived two different lives – the busy, active one at Evergreen Heights and the quiet, reclusive life on Hushed Hollow Road.

In some ways, I didn't really mind, though. I felt I was an easy-going kid, and I could understand dad's busyness. So, if no one had time to play ball with me at his house, I found other ways to keep myself entertained. For the times when I ran out of ideas, I knew Grammy and Grampy Miller were just down the road. I could always walk down to their house when I got bored. The rule was that I call dad once I got there so he knew I had arrived safely. Being a rural, country road, there was very little traffic, so safety wasn't a huge concern. There was also very little chance that I would be kidnapped or struck by a car. This was rural farm country.

Grammy Miller always had fresh-baked cookies waiting for me, almost as though she knew I would be walking through the door at any minute to lay claim to one or two of them. Plus, when I went to her house, she let me watch anything I wanted to on her TV. I didn't have to fight for control of the remote. Grampy Miller always acted as though he was interested in my animated kid shows, but I often caught him watching television with his eyes closed.

If life had had a bumpy start, it seemed to have mellowed out now. Things were going super good. I loved my busy family at mom's house, and although dad's house was always quiet, sometimes I looked forward to the change. The tranquility offset the busy atmosphere of my "Brady Bunch" family. I had grown used to the routine of drifting back and forth between homes, and I knew what to expect.

During the winter time when it was too cold to play outside and our beach days were on hold, we would play board games around the dining room table. Frequently, my stepsiblings would be there and we would form teams to play against each other. At other times, we would play a family game of charades in the living room, which was always good for a laugh. Then there were times when we played Scrabble or Yahtzee. I remember one time when I tried to cheat at Yahtzee. I rolled the dice intentionally close to the edge of the coffee table so it would fall onto the floor.

"Yahtzee!" I called in victory. But nobody believed me, and they weren't going to let me off that easily.

"Prove it," Big Jake insisted.

I held up the dice, showing the exact number I needed to match the rest of the dice.

"Do you think we were born yesterday?" he asked. "You cheated and we all know it. Roll them again!"

No way were they going to let me win through cheating. If I wanted to win, I had to play by the rules. So, I rolled the dice again, and of course, I didn't get a Yahtzee. It was a good effort, though!

The one game that stood out the most in my memory was the Sunday afternoon when we decided to play Scrabble. Alicia was only seven, but she wanted to be an active participant. We tried to explain the need to be able to read and spell as a prerequisite to playing the game, but she insisted she could. Not wanting her to feel left out, we suggested she form a team with her older sister, Mariah. They had a few years between them, which left Mariah older, more mature, and better at spelling. The girls were agreeable to the arrangement, so the game began.

At one point, when it was their turn, Alicia got all excited. Looking at the board and then back at her letters, she eagerly said, "I got it, Mariah. Let me do this one."

She promptly laid the letters "s-h-a-y" down on the board and grinned with satisfaction. The rest of us stared at the board in confusion, trying to figure out what she had just done. When we failed to comprehend her word, we turned our confused gazes her way. She was still beaming, as proud as any peacock could be, excited that she had just formed her own word.

Finally, Paul looked at her and said, "I give up, honey. What does that spell?"

It never dawned on her that if nobody could figure it out, then maybe it wasn't really a word. She just jubilantly piped up and said, "Shay – like shay ships."

We knew she had a bit of a speech problem, but we thought it was cute and she would eventually outgrow it. We would gently try to correct her when she pronounced something incorrectly, but at the same time smiled at her sweet innocence. However, at this particular moment, her innocence left us baffled.

It was my mom who finally figured it out. "Oh, I know!" she said, waving her hands in excitement. "You mean like potato chips."

"Yah," she nodded, like it all made perfect sense. "That's what I said – shay ships."

Everyone laughed hysterically. It was true – she did call them "shay ships." In fact, "shay ships" were her all-time favorite snack. Someday, she would learn to read and write correctly, and would realize they were actually potato chips, but today she was pleased with "shay."

From that day on, her nickname became Shay. It was a defining moment that brought us all closer together, and she seemed to like her new name. Little Shay was just a lovable, adorable girl. She was sweet and innocent, and forever eager to please. If she could make you laugh, well, that was all the better. She liked being a bright spot in everybody's life.

While I admired my older brothers and adored Little Ricky and Nicole, I found that Little Shay had a way of warming your heart. Her smile alone was enough to make you smile in return. She had such simple beauty to her, a happiness in life that you don't often find in people. She was pleased to be alive, and wanted to share her contentment in life with anyone who crossed her path. You rarely heard her complain about anything.

I will never forget the time we went kite flying in the park. She quickly got bored, and tired of holding the kite string, but she didn't want to quit when everyone else still seemed to be having fun. So, she tied the kite string to her lawn chair and wandered off to play with Ricky and Nicole.

Shortly thereafter, she was spotted chasing her lawn chair across the baseball field. Her kite had apparently picked up a tailwind, and seemed to be heading into outer space. She was running for all she was worth, trying to catch up to her runaway chair. While Paul ran to help her, we all laughed as we watched her, almost as hard as we had laughed at the Scrabble game when she had acquired her nickname. She was a real joy to have around, and always seemed to keep us laughing. She had a sweet, naïve nature to her. She rarely got mad at anyone. If they said something that sounded degrading to her, she would just smile and laugh. She always took things as a joke, and never took anything to heart.

Of course, she was a bit of a practical joker, too. Like the time we went bike riding and she wiped out. My mom and stepdad were walking in the park while the rest of us were riding bikes on the bike path. Little Shay was not known for her coordination, so we were not surprised when she lost control of her bike and flipped over. We were all within sight of each other, so her fall was observed by most of us. However, after falling, she failed to get up.

We all ran to her in horror. Something must be terribly wrong. Had she lost consciousness? Was she so hurt that she couldn't move? She didn't seem to be crying, but she wasn't moving either. As fast as we ran, it still seemed to take forever to get to her. And when we did, she rolled over, smiled up at us, and said, "Got you!!"

She apparently hadn't been injured, but wanted to trick us all into thinking that she was. That little monster! She had just scared the wits out of us, yet she got up laughing about it. To Little Shay, everything was happy time. Life, to her, was just one big joke.

****

Life with my Rapini family was great. No, actually, it was awesome. Oh, sure, there were some bumps along the way. No family is ever perfect. My stepfather lost his job and decided to start a new career. It meant time out-of-state for the initial training, and I was happy to act as the man of the house while he was away. I asked my dad if I could stay at my mother's house while Paul was away, and was surprised when he agreed to it.

Even though I missed my stepfather and our family outings, I enjoyed myself while he was gone. Since it was winter time, I found plenty of work to do. I kept busy with shoveling the driveway and cleaning the snow off my mom's car. I would do my best to entertain my younger siblings, like taking them out to play in the snow or playing games inside if it was too chilly to be outside.

During those months, Little Ricky got terribly sick with tonsillitis. His little cheeks were rosy red, and it was easy to see that he didn't feel good. While my mom was occupied with housework, I would keep an eye on him. He would stay on the couch, and we would either watch TV together or play some video games.

I always made sure he had something cold to drink or a Popsicle to suck on, hoping it would help his throat to feel better. And when his face looked like he was burning up, I would get a cool cloth for his forehead. I sat with him diligently for days, until he was finally better.

My mother really appreciated all my help during those months. She would rub my head or back, maybe give me a quick hug and say, "You are so good to us, Jakie Jr. Thank you for all your help. You have such a good heart. Maybe we should call you Jakie Goodheart instead!" My mom had a way of making me feel special and needed.

****

My stepfather had finally made it home and everything returned to normal, or as normal as a family like ours could be. Of course, there were the occasional sibling squabbles that all families experience. There was always the chaos of who was sleeping at which house and when, but I was happy with my life. Things were going well, and I wouldn't have wanted to change anything.

Yes, maybe my childhood had encountered a rough start, but it had mellowed out and everything was good again. I was finally standing on solid ground, and I was satisfied with life. I had been given a second chance at my childhood and, for that, I was extremely grateful. On one hand, I was anxious to grow up and become independent, just as any child dreams about. Yet, on the other hand, I secretly hoped things would never change.

CHAPTER 3
A Life Cut Short

They say that all good things must come to an end, but I didn't know it would end so soon. Life had been awesome since my stepsiblings had walked into my world. Even though we sometimes bickered or argued, we were always quick to patch things up. We only had a couple of weekends a month together, so we didn't want to stay mad for long. Plus, we got along too well to stay angry, anyway. Who had time for that?

As hard as I tried to not play favorites, I couldn't help myself. Little Ricky worshiped the ground that I walked on and followed me around like I was a super hero. How could you help but love someone like that? And Little Shay had such a pure zest for life that she always made me smile.

Oh, sure, my other siblings held special places in my heart, too. But Ricky and Shay were the cream of the crop, the lights of my life, the ones who always put a smile on my face. The room would light up when they walked into it. Or maybe that's just how they made me feel every time I saw them. Anyway, since I was their big brother, I did all that I could to protect them and return the love they so freely gave to me.

Then one day, late in the school year, I realized how human I was and how little protection I could provide for my younger siblings. It was a tragedy that brought our world crashing down. And not just for me, but for my whole Rapini family. Who could have known such a beautiful, warm, late spring day would end so tragically.

We were all excited that winter had passed and school would soon be out for the summer. Life was full of expectation. We were looking forward to more days at Sandy Beach, swimming and barbequing, plus trips to the park to fly kites and ride bikes. The days we dreamed of all winter long of being outside, enjoying nature, and sharing quality family time together were finally here. Summer time had always been our favorite time of the year.

Yet, that summer would be one of the hardest seasons, not just of the year, but of our entire lives. Little Shay was almost a teenager, and she naturally wanted to do teenage things. This particular day involved the teenage trait of skipping school. There were only a few weeks left of school anyway, so what would one day matter? Her friends were having a party, and she wanted to go. She was staying at her mother's house, and who knows if her mother was even aware of her plans. But Little Shay made the wrong choice that day, and her happy-go-lucky innocence and naïve nature proved to be her downfall.

There is probably no way anyone could have foreseen what was about to happen. It was a freak accident, quite honestly. Just a bunch of kids, hanging out, wanting to experiment with feeling high. Oh, they weren't doing anything illegal. It's not like they were doing drugs or anything. They were just partying at a friend's house, sniffing household chemicals, and waiting for some kind of a buzz. But unfortunately, Little Shay's body couldn't tolerate the chemical she had inhaled.

Some of the kids passed out after inhaling whatever substance they found, so when Shay passed out, nobody was really alarmed. Plus, everyone knew what a practical joker she was anyway. Maybe she was just faking. However, when she failed to regain consciousness, they started to grow concerned. By then, it was too late for Little Shay. Her youthful body had grown lifeless, and there was nothing anyone could do to help her. The ambulance had been called and, as hard as the medical technicians tried, there was just no saving her.

For months, our family was numb, and it was a struggle just to get through our daily activities. Little Shay was gone. That's all our brains could handle for the time being. How could this have happened? Why did someone so sweet and innocent, someone who had such enthusiasm for life, have to leave the thing she loved so much? What was the purpose of taking one so young, and good, and decent?

She would have made a wonderful mother, an awesome aunt, an unbelievable grandmother. Yet, she would never experience any of these. In fact, she wasn't even afforded the opportunity to be a teenager. She would never be a cheerleader, never go to any football games, would not make it to her high school prom. She would never feel the pride and accomplishment of graduating from school, and she would never hold her father's arm to walk down the aisle at her wedding, or share her life with the man she loved. Little Shay was gone, and her leaving left a massive hole in all of our hearts.

Night after night, I would lie in my bed and think of her. I thought of the last time we were together as a family, before my stepfather had left for his training. We had gone ice skating at the town park. Someone had left a milk crate in the snow beside the rink, probably to sit on while they laced their skates. Little Shay had dragged it onto the ice, and we had taken turns pushing her around on it. She had been a real comedian, as usual, throwing her arms wide and letting out a "whoop" as she sailed across the ice.

Now she was gone, never to return. One wild, school skipping, chemical-sniffing party had ended it all for her. I couldn't get over how the thing she had loved the most - life itself - had been snatched away. One day we were a happy, fun-loving family and the next, we were lost, confused, and broken. Our hearts were shattered, and life suddenly seemed hollow and empty.

The best way to describe what happened was to compare it to viewing life through a large, plate glass window. I had seen everything I wanted through this window. It was full of life and color. There were people in this window who loved me and wanted to spend time with me. It was an active, healthy, fun-filled childhood where we were making wonderful, vibrant memories. Then, all at once, a meteor had crashed through it and changed everything. My bright, colorful, brilliant life had turned into a dark, gloomy world of despair and discouragement.

I didn't know it then, but that was just the beginning of my heartache. The loss of one so young and unexpectedly can leave a family reeling, and mine was not without exception. We tried to go through the rituals, tried to do all the things we used to do, but they just weren't the same anymore. We all carried a weight in our hearts that left us lagging. The joy we had shared as a family was gone. It was like her death had broken a link in the chain that held us together. We were struggling to find a way to pull that chain back together again and mend the broken link, but nobody knew how.

It hit my stepfather the hardest, though. While he was away, he had trained to become a paramedic, and he beat up on himself over her death. He was sure that if he had been there, he could have saved her. It wasn't until he hired a private detective to investigate her death that my parents truly understood what had happened. Then he finally accepted that he probably couldn't have done anything to revive his daughter. She had had an instantaneous physical reaction to the chemical she had inhaled, and no human intervention could have saved her.

That doesn't mean he accepted her death, though. The heartache proved to be too much for him. He couldn't continue to live in the same area without her, seeing the places he used to take her. Driving past the park was excruciating for him, realizing he would never take her kite flying, bike riding, or skating there again. Sandy Beach was especially hard. He tried for a while to continue the family outings to the beach, but his heart wasn't in it. The memories were too fresh, and the void left by Shay's passing was too real.

All he wanted was to go back to his childhood home, to live closer to his mother, and to start over again. That was several hours and a few states away from where we currently lived. My mother didn't want to leave, but he clearly didn't plan on staying. So, he packed his belongings and moved out.

My mom did all she could to try to hold our family together. I know that now, but at the time I didn't understand. She stayed in her house down the road from us at Evergreen Heights for as long as possible, and commuted back and forth between home and her husband. Yet, it wasn't long before it took its toll on her. It was simply too much driving, and something she could not continue to do. She had to make a choice and, having had one marriage fail, she wanted to do all she could to save the second one.

Her choice broke my heart even more. She chose to follow her husband and move away. I was losing my mother again. For the second time, she was walking out of my life, but this time, she was not just down the road like before. It wasn't like I could stop by to visit her every other weekend. She would be gone, and I would have to be satisfied with just talking to her on the phone.

I begged her to take me with her. Maybe our family life wasn't what it had been, but I hoped that maybe we could revive it. I knew my Rapini stepsiblings wouldn't be there, but I needed my mother. If I lost her, the hole in my heart would only grow bigger. She had to take me, too. I didn't care that I would have to go to a different school and make new friends. Little Ricky and Nicole would have to do the same thing. We could all be there for each other.

It seemed as though my plea fell on deaf ears, but I knew it wasn't completely her decision. She wanted me to go with her, but my dad wouldn't allow it. He didn't want another man to raise his son, and he wanted me close enough to be an active part of his life. The move was just too far away to allow that. It would be too challenging to commute back and forth for visits. Even though it broke my heart, my father won the battle and I settled back into our home at Hushed Hollow Road.

I was older this time, but I didn't handle my mom's leaving any better than I had the first time. Sleeping became extremely difficult. I couldn't shut my brain off at night when I wanted to sleep, and I found myself lying in bed thinking about Little Shay, wondering where her sweet little spirit had gone. When I wasn't thinking about her, I was thinking about my mother and how much I missed her. Not just my mom, though, I missed all of my siblings and the life we had built together. Life at Hushed Hollow Road was just what its name implied. It was very quiet there, hushed like the sound of a library. Plus, it seemed so very hollow, without the joy and laughter I had shared with all my siblings.

I wanted to cry myself to sleep every night, just like in my younger days. But teenage boys aren't supposed to cry. I knew it wouldn't solve anything anyway. This time was different. I hadn't lost just my mother. I had lost Little Shay forever. I had lost the stepsiblings I had come to love. They went to live full-time with their mother, while my sister, Kelli and I, had gone back to live with my dad. And my mother took Little Ricky and Nicole with her when she left. We were now three separate families and would live in three separate worlds.

I had hoped and prayed night after night that God would help us pull our family back together. Yet, when the sale of my mother's house had finalized, I knew it was for real. It was a dark day in my memory. They were really leaving.

The day they packed up and moved away had been incredibly painful. Watching what was left of my family drive away on that fateful day had almost broken my heart completely in two. I had given Little Ricky an extended hug, not wanting to ever let go of him. I knew if I let him go, I might not see him again for a very long time. Although he was young, he sensed the sorrow, too. He waved until the car disappeared out of sight.

****

It was all gone now. The quiet days at my dad's house became my normal routine and life as I now knew it. My grandparents were still down the road, and welcomed me any time I wanted to come visit. I knew my mother was just hours away, but it might as well have been in a foreign country. It's not like I could just hop in a car and go see her any time I chose, or stay for the weekends like before.

I desperately missed all my Rapini family and our fun times together. I longed for the trips to the park to fly kites and ride bikes. I would dream about the outings at the beach and our family barbeques we had enjoyed so much. I felt like I only had half a life now. The other half had vanished, simply faded away, and left me with a massive black hole in my world. Since my stepsiblings had gone back to live with their mother in another town, we didn't even get to see them at school. The Rapini family was spread out over different states, and much too far apart to come together again.

I tried to salvage part of my life and suggested my dad call me Jakie, Jr., yet I knew it was just a fantasy. He was too formal for games like that. He called me Jacob, like he always had, or Jacob Paul when I was out of line. He said that "Jakie" was a child's nickname. Now that I was getting older, it was time for me to be mature and act more like a man. It was almost as though "Jakie, Jr." had died when Little Shay did. He just didn't seem to exist anymore.

I never realized how fragile life could be. I was just a juvenile who thought life was supposed to be fun, exciting, and full of adventure. Like most immature kids, I took everything for granted and just assumed it would all be there tomorrow morning when I woke up. Just another day, ready for whatever quest might come my way. My biggest concerns had been what to eat for breakfast and what I was going to do after school. Now that had all changed, and life wasn't so simple anymore.

****

Even with the emptiness and heartache in my life, I found a way to move on. What choice did I have? It wasn't like I could stop living just because Shay had. Every morning I would wake up and start another day. I knew my siblings hurt as much as I did, so I told myself if they could go on, then I could, too. But it didn't take away the pain or make life any easier to bear. We were in "survival" mode now, trying to make it successfully through each day.

Just as I had suspected, even though my mother and siblings were only a matter of hours away, it was difficult to get together to see them. Sometimes, we would meet in the middle, but rarely did either of us ever go all the way to spend more than just a few hours together. Only twice did I get to go for an overnight visit. It was just too hard to coordinate schedules and find time to be together.

As before, I found a way to adjust and accept my fate in life. My friends at school became my extended family. I would hang out with them when I wanted something to do, and it's not like I didn't have any family time. It was just different from before.

My father was not one to go to the park or the beach. He liked to stay at home, and very rarely left the house other than to run errands and work. His interests in his spare time were hunting and guns. So, my family time became learning how to shoot and doing target practice with him in the back yard.

I found I was really interested in guns. They were fascinating and powerful, and I discovered that I handled them well. My dad even commented on what a good aim I was while we were doing target practice. He was a man of few words, so a word of praise from him went a long way. He told me when I felt confident and ready, we could go hunting together.

He had always been a hunter, but I had never really shared his interest. But, now with the other half of my family gone and a lot of free time on my hands, I became more interested in the aspect of giving it a try. I wasn't sure I would be brave enough to actually shoot a live animal, but I enjoyed firing a gun. Even if I didn't hit my target, it was still quality time spent with my dad. Most of the time, he was so busy around the house, or at work, that we didn't spend a lot of time together.

When I wasn't doing target practice with my dad, I would find little things to keep me busy. We had a garage, and he let me use a corner of it to set up a little workshop. I started collecting tools, and used them to tinker on bikes, the lawn mower, or anything that seemed like it needed repair. I didn't necessarily know what I was doing, but I thought I could learn as I worked. Plus, it gave me something to fill the void.

And, of course, there were always video games to play and computers to utilize. I know I spent way too much time looking at a screen, but it wasn't like I had a lot of other things to keep me occupied. We didn't have any neighbors to hang out with, Little Ricky and my siblings lived too far away to hang out with, and I didn't have a license to go anywhere. So, most of my time was spent doing target practice, tinkering in the garage, or watching some screen somewhere. If I got bored with all that, I would wander down the road to visit my grandparents.

It was almost like I was on my third life. My first life was the few short years where my family was intact and we were what I considered the perfect family – Mom, Dad, Kelli and me. When that changed, I had thought life was over. Yet, it had revived itself when my mom married Paul, and my second life began. That was an awesome life, and even though it was over, I was thankful for the memories. Now, I was into a new chapter, an entirely different phase of my life. I could only wonder where the next chapter would lead me, and contemplated if this was the way my entire life would go. Maybe I was like a cat and would be granted nine lives. But was that really what I wanted for myself?

CHAPTER 4
Life Goes On

They say the teenage years are hard, and I guess I would have to agree with that. They are full of important decisions that can affect the rest of your life. As I think back on those years, I often wonder how my life would have been different if my mother had been there to offer some guidance.

Oh, it's not like I was a wild, out-of-control teenager. I did a few things that I regret, but what teenager doesn't? We all make poor choices at some point in our lives. But even as the days dragged on, I still missed my mom and often wished I could come home to see her standing in the kitchen. As I walked home from the bus stop, I would day dream about walking into the house and find her waiting for me. In my mind, she would turn to look at me as I entered the kitchen, smile with a look of adoration on her face, and ask me how my day went. And then she would hold out a plateful of cookies that she had baked for me while I was away.

I knew it was foolish to torture myself with visions like that. My mother was gone, and there was nothing I could do about it. Maybe she wasn't gone as permanently as Little Shay, but she was no longer an active part of my life. She wasn't there to attend my award ceremonies at school. She wasn't there to congratulate me on any of my accomplishments. Other kids would be annoyed at ball games to see their mothers cheering them from the stands, but I longed to look over and find my mother watching me, shouting words of encouragement to me. I longed to hear her voice call out, "That a boy, Jakie, Jr.! You can do this!" But the voice was never there.

Oh, sure, I could call her on the phone and hear her voice then, but it wasn't the same. I wanted to see the facial expressions that come with a mother's love, or just share an occasional hug. Talking on the phone didn't allow me to see the look of pride on her face at some great accomplishment I had achieved. It didn't afford me the feel of her embrace, or let me see physical clues to be reassured that she really did love me and was pleased that she had given birth to me.

On the days when the visions became too much for me, I would walk down to visit my grandmother. She always had that plateful of cookies for me. She would give me the hugs I longed for, or have that look of pride on her face that I needed to see. If I hadn't been so close to my grandmother, I probably would have given up long before I did. She was the glue that held me together throughout my difficult teenage years. I could always count on her support and reassurance that life was good and I was loved.

As with any other teenage boy, I became fascinated with the girls at school. One of them caught my eye at an early age. Jacki was an amazing girl. I couldn't help but get jittery when she was around, and thought how cute it would sound to become a couple. Together, we could be Jakie and Jacki.

I would have given anything to be brave enough to ask her out, but I couldn't find the nerve. I was so afraid she would say no, and I didn't think I could handle the rejection. With all the losses I had faced in my life, being discarded by someone as beautiful as she was would probably have destroyed me. So instead, I admired her from a distance.

However, Amanda was a different story. She had a crush on me, and she didn't mind letting me know. It seemed that every time I turned around, Amanda was there. It's not like she was stalking me, really. It's just that she found ways to make sure our paths crossed frequently.

Her eyes and quick smile told me of her interest, so I felt safe in asking her out. I didn't think she would turn me down and leave me feeling foolish for the attempt. And, as I expected, she was quick to accept my offer. She would love to go out with me, she said. Just let her know when and where, and she would be there.

That day I didn't walk home from school, I floated. A girl at school was actually interested in dating me! I wanted so much to run home and tell someone, but I didn't think anyone there would really care. I knew it wouldn't mean much to my dad, and Kelli would probably tease me about having a girlfriend. So I didn't tell anyone about it and kept it to myself. Maybe I would walk down to Grammy Miller's house tomorrow and let her know, but for today, it was my secret.

****

Even though I had felt I could never recover from my mother leaving me for a second time, I found that I finally made it past "survival mode" and managed to adjust and move on with my life. School was going well, and

Amanda and I grew closer every day. Not only did we see each other during the day at school, but she would call me every night as well. Sometimes our parents would allow us to spend a few hours together on a school night, and we always got together on at least one day over the weekend.

Transportation proved to be an issue, though. Not only was it a rural area, but Amanda lived in another town, and neither of us had a driver's license. But I had always been good at problem solving, so together we came up with a plan. If we joined after school activities, we could spend more time together. In the fall, she would play soccer and I would stay after school to cheer her on. In the spring, I would sign up for baseball, and she would be there for me. Finally, after years of hoping and dreaming, I had someone sitting on the bleachers cheering for me. It was like a dream come true.

We also joined the Mentor's Club, which held sessions throughout the school year. It was an after school program designed to help younger children, but it benefited us as well. We would walk to the Elementary School twice a week to help the younger children with strength building skills. Our role was to help them with homework, and then provide a fun activity as a reward for getting it done.

Some days our activity would just be a supervised free play on the school playground. Other days, we would do fun activities like arts and craft projects, scavenger hunts, or physical fitness activities like jump roping contests or races around the playground. We also taught them about nutrition and developing good problem-solving skills. The program managers allowed us to help develop the curriculum and accepted any ideas we could think of to help shape the children into well-rounded, healthy individuals.

It proved to be a fun program, not just for the children, but for Amanda and me as well. Walking from one school to another gave us time to talk, and frequently Amanda would reach over and hold my hand while we walked. I often felt more like I was floating than walking. Just the warmth of her hand in mine made me feel wanted and accepted like I had never known before. Someone actually loved me enough to hold my hand in public places.

While I enjoyed the sports we both played, it was the Mentor's Club that we looked forward to the most. It wasn't just because it allowed us to spend time together, though. More than that, it was a worthwhile program that helped the children in many ways, and also gave us a sense of purpose. Often when I looked across the cafeteria or playground, I would find Amanda watching me over the heads of the children. It always surprised me that she was so aware of my whereabouts, and it always excited me to know she was keeping an eye on me.

****

My relationship with Amanda seemed to grow deeper every day. And things improved at home with my dad, too. For my sixteenth birthday, he bought me an ATV. It wasn't a new machine, but it was good enough for me. I was ecstatic! It was the best gift he had ever given me. I almost wore the grass out, circling around the house and through the fields out back. Listening to me roar around the house, he probably regretted buying it for me. But he never complained about it. He probably felt that at least it kept me close to home, so he knew where I was, and also kept me out of trouble. His only rules were to wear a helmet and stay off the front lawn.

When I wasn't with Amanda, riding my ATV, tinkering around my workshop, or glued to some screen somewhere, I would work on my target practice. Sometimes, Dad would come out and shoot with me. He taught me how to clean and care for guns. Then, when he felt I was doing well with my target practice, he brought me to the local gun store and allowed me to pick out a rifle.

Learning to fire a rifle was different. I had to remember to watch for the kickback so I wouldn't acquire a shoulder injury. I will admit that I did end up with a bruise or two before I finally learned to keep it snuggled tightly against my shoulder. I have never been a quitter, though, so I per- sisted, even with the bruises. I was motivated by my dad promising to take me hunting once I had mastered the rifle.

Amanda hated guns, so I avoided the target practice when she was around. That activity could be a special thing between my dad and me. It allowed us to bond in a way we never had before. And Amanda was more interested in the ATV, anyway. She loved riding around the yard with me, and would ride behind me for what seemed like hours while we circled around the yard. Sometimes, we would pack a lunch and ride the ATV into the woods for a picnic.

If we were counting lives, Amanda seemed to consume my fourth one. And it was going pretty well, in fact. The pain of losing Little Shay, along with having my mom, Little Ricky, and Nicole leaving was still there, but it faded a bit with the newfound love that I had with Amanda. I longed to share details of my love for Amanda with my mother and get advice from her, but it didn't seem appropriate over the phone. And it was noth- ing my dad was interested in talking about. He had never gotten past losing my mother, so relationship advice was just not his expertise. Plus, he had always been a private person who didn't like to talk about matters of the heart.

There were times when I would confide in Kelli a bit, but she was having her own relationship issues, and I didn't want her to be jealous that I was so happy with mine. Grammy Miller was anxious to meet Amanda, and I knew at some point I would need to bring her down and introduce her to my grandparents, but I wasn't ready for that yet. I still wanted to keep her to myself and bask in the fact that she was mine.

I had a girlfriend, and she didn't care if I was Jakie, Jr., Jacob Paul Miller, or even Frankenstein. She loved me for who I was, and that was something I had longed for all my life.

****

Amanda, or Mandi, as she became known to my family, became a welcomed wonder to my world. She brought a new zest for life to me. Mandi seemed to breathe life into the cavities of my soul that had been empty for a very long time. No longer did I wake up with a sense of dread each morning. Instead, I awoke happy and anxious to face the new day.

Every morning I held high expectations, wondering what blissful event would happen that day. I hadn't felt that way in years, not since before Little Shay had died or my Rapini family had become part of my life. The dark, empty caverns of my inner being were once again filled with light.

In the spring of our junior year at high school, we were both able to acquire our driver's licenses. It was such a blessing to no longer be compromised by transportation issues. Because of this, it was not unusual to look across the dinner table and see her smiling back at me. Plus, Dad didn't mind the extra company. Kelli had since graduated from high school and moved in with our mom, wanting to attend a college near her. This had left a void in our household, and Mandi's presence helped to fill that emptiness.

Long ago, I had mustered up the courage to bring her over to meet my grandparents. If I had had any doubts that they wouldn't like her, they immediately faded at our first introduction. Grammy Miller welcomed her with open arms. Her philosophy was that if I loved Mandi, than that was good enough for her. She would love Mandi, too.

The next couple of years seemed to fly by with lightning speed. Maybe it was because we were at the end of our years of formal schooling, and there were lots of activities to participate in. Or maybe just because we were in love and we floated through the years. Whatever the case may have been, we soon found ourselves walking across the platform at our high school graduation, flipping our tassels, and anxious to take on the world.

I hadn't seen my mother for quite some time, but with Mandi around, the pain of missing her hadn't been so severe. Mandi kept me busy, entertained, and happy. Hanging out with Mandi made me forget some of the pains of the past. The void left by my losses had finally faded. My life now had purpose, along with something to look forward to each day. And now that we had graduated from high school, life was full of endless possibilities.

One thing that had troubled me a bit about Amanda, though, was her tendency to be jealous. Throughout our school days, she had hovered over me. If she saw me talking to another girl, she automatically became suspicious. I had always had girls that were friends. But that's all they were, and I thought we both knew that. However, if Amanda knew that any of my "girl" friends had called me or if she saw us talking in the hallway, she would question me about it later.

In a way, it had annoyed me. They had always been my friends, and I didn't see the need to end a relationship because I was dating Amanda. Yet, on the other hand, it was kind of cool that someone was jealous about me. She wanted me all to herself, and it felt so good to be wanted. And now that school was over, it didn't seem like it should be an issue any more. It would be just me and Mandi, our future together, and whatever that might hold. As happy as I felt when she was around, I could only imagine how bright our future would be. We seemed to be a match made to last, and I felt life could only get better.

CHAPTER 5
On Our Own

I couldn't believe school was over and we were starting a new life together. There were so many options in life. Which paths would Mandi and I take? What careers would we choose? Where would we live? That first summer after school ended, we would lie in the backyard under the stars at night and talk about our future, our dreams, and the endless possibilities.

Since computers had always fascinated me, I decided to pursue a degree in Computer Sciences at the local technical college. Mandi decided it would make sense if we both attended the same college, so she applied for the nursing program. My dad was willing to let us stay with him for awhile until we were financially secure enough to get a place of our own. He said the house was big enough for the three of us, and he didn't mind having company for a few more years.

Marriage wasn't on our To-Do List yet, though. We had talked a bit about it, but it wasn't something we were ready to take on. We were still young and needed to get our feet planted a little more firmly on the ground. It was our place to focus on our schooling before we were ready to take on a commitment as important as that. So, off to school we went, again.

College was much more fun and exciting than high school had been. Maybe it was because we were learning about something we were really interested in, instead of studying things that didn't mean much to us – like geometry and biology. I was fascinated with computers and electronics, and how they all worked. I loved learning, tackled each course with fervor and anticipation, and was actually disappointed upon the completion of each semester.

Mandi had enjoyed her nursing program as much as I had savored the computer technology training. Before we knew it, we had completed our two year programs and found ourselves ready to walk across the stage to accept our diplomas. I made sure my mom and Kelli knew about graduation night, and they had agreed to come. I hadn't seen either of them for quite some time, and I was very excited at the thought of them attending the ceremony.

Finally, graduation night arrived, and I watched anxiously for my mom's arrival. Soon, I saw Kelli entering the auditorium. I looked around to see my mother, but couldn't seem to locate her. Kelli was walking in with a group of people, but the lady directly behind her didn't stir any waves of familiarity.

I hurried over to give her a hug, and was about to ask where mom was when the lady with her reached over and gave me a hug.

"I'm so proud of you, sweetie," she whispered in my ear.

It was like a jolt of electricity shot through my body, and I instantly pulled back for a second look. It was my mother! It had been so long since I had seen her, I didn't even recognize her. She had dyed her hair a lighter shade of blonde and had lost a lot of weight. The only thing that struck a cord of recognition with me was her voice.

A whirlwind of emotions exploded inside of me. At first, shock and disbelief hit me. How could a child not know their own mother, the person who had given birth to them? It seemed that no matter how long it had been since I had seen her, I was confident that I would have known her in an instant.

However, the shock quickly gave way to a feeling of joy and elation. I couldn't believe she had actually come. I had feared she wouldn't be able to fit my graduation into her busy schedule, and yet here she was. So many of my childhood milestones she had missed, and I had needed to rely on my dad or my Miller grandparents to be the support system.

Unfortunately, that memory triggered a bit of anger, which was a well of frustration housed deep inside of me. Where had she been for my challenging teenage years when I could have used some motherly advice and nurturing? Plus, all of my school events that should have been a time of celebration for me had always been a feeling of emptiness because she wasn't there.

I knew I couldn't dwell on this last emotion, or it would spoil the feeling of accomplishment that I was entitled to for tonight. I looked past her and cried out in unbelief. Little Ricky was standing behind her. He was as tall as I was, and not so little anymore, but I would have recognized him anywhere. Looking past him, I saw Nicole and even Paul, too. She had brought the whole family! I couldn't remember the last time we had been together. Now, they had all come for me. My Rapini family was here to celebrate my special event!

    That proved to be one very special day for me, much better than my high school graduation had been. I felt as though I floated across the stage, knowing that my whole family was out there cheering for me. Not just my dad with Grammy and Grampy Miller, but this time, my mom, and Kelli, along with Little Ricky, Nicole, and Paul. I thought I would burst with joy, and wanted to run across the stage, or jump up and down when I received my diploma. However, I held myself back, walking proud and true, proving to them how mature I had become.

    After the graduation ceremony, we went out for pizza, and then the Rapini portion of my family spent the night. My parents had planned a bigger celebration for the next day, in which they had invited extended family.

    I couldn't believe it the next day when car after car pulled into the yard to come celebrate my achievement. My maternal grandparents came, along with aunts, uncles, and cousins from both sides. The biggest surprise, though, was when my Rapini step-siblings showed up. I hadn't seen them since the day my mother had moved away, more years ago than I cared to think about.

    What a day it proved to be! Ricky and I quickly made up for lost time. He was fascinated with my ATV, so we spent a good portion of the day circling around the yard over and over. It was like we had just seen each other yesterday. All the years of being apart melted away, and we were just two siblings sharing quality time together, enjoying the presence of each other.

    If I had felt my family didn't care about me, it all changed that day. With so many of my loved ones coming to share this special experience with me, it proved that they did love me, even if we weren't together. Time and distance may have kept us apart, but the family ties were still there. I cherished the memories of that extraordinary day for a very long time.

    However, the fact that I hadn't recognized my own mother troubled me for quite some time. How is it possible for a child to not know their own mother? A bond between a mother and child should be so strong that one would think they would know their own mother anywhere. Yet, I hadn't even recognized her. We had spent way too many years apart. I vowed to try to keep that from happening in the future. We both needed to make more of an effort to stay in touch.

****

Following graduation from college, it didn't take long for Mandi and me to acquire successful positions in the work force. After a few months of full-time, steady employment, we decided to get a place of our own. We saved up our money for a security deposit and started searching for an apartment. We decided to move into a nearby town named Newton Falls and begin our new life together there, as a couple who was independent and on our own.

I couldn't believe how good life was. I had a woman who loved me. We both had successful careers with respectable incomes, and now we had an apartment of our own. This newfound freedom was great, and I was loving every minute of it. There was only one thing that seemed to be missing, though — a dog. I had always wanted a dog of my own, but it was not something my father would allow in his house.

Oh, sure, maybe getting married would have perfected the equation, but I still wasn't ready for that yet. I knew that I loved Mandi. However, there were a couple of things that held me back. One was that she had been my only girlfriend, and I wasn't convinced that you could find your soul mate and lifetime partner on the first try.

The other issue was that she never stirred emotions within me like Jacki had in high school. To me, Jacki was just plain amazing. Every time I had seen her, it was like she electrified my body. I would sometimes actually jump when I laid eyes on her. I guess you could say it was a real "knock-your-socks-off" kind of feeling. She had always made me feel giddy, nervous, and tongue-tied when I saw her.

Mandi didn't do that to me. Hers was a steady love, a dependable love, one that made me feel cherished and needed in return. It was a friendship that had grown stronger with time and developed into a loving relationship. We felt comfortable together and definitely needed each other, but our relationship had never made my head spin, like being around Jacki did. So for now, marriage didn't seem to fit the picture, but adding a dog seemed appropriate.

Mandi was okay with the idea of a pet. Her family had been pet owners, and she thought getting a dog was a great idea. So, we started our search, and it wasn't long before we had an addition to our family. Rex was a rescue dog. He was a pure mutt, but a clever dog, and a very lovable little guy. He blended into the family nicely.

When Mandi and I weren't working, you could frequently find us at the dog park, playing ball with Rex or just taking him for a walk. It made me sad to think of all the years I had missed out on not having a pet. Maybe it could have helped to fill the void of losing Little Shay and my Rapini family. It might have aided in bringing comfort to all those lonely nights when I lay in bed, pining for my lost family and fighting hard to not cry myself to sleep. Just think how comforting a pet could have been. Rex gave an unconditional love that I could have used during those dark, lonely nights.

Those days were in the past, though. It was something I told myself often. Life was too good now to focus on the shortcomings of days gone by. In fact, with Rex around, it was like we had our own little "Rapini" family. We would take him with us on hikes, weekend camping trips, and to every family gathering. We spent a lot of time with Mandi's family, since they lived closer than mine. Kelli was still living with my mother and Paul, and the distance made it difficult to spend time together, even though I had promised myself I would spend more time with them. A busy work schedule and the traveling distance between us always seemed to get in the way.

I kept in touch with local family, though. My dad and I would go hunting frequently. Since he had taught me the love of guns and how to shoot, our hunting days became an opportunity to spend quality time together. We shared few things in common, but he loved guns and hunting as much as I did. Even if we didn't find anything to shoot, it was always an enjoyable way to spend time together out in nature.

Grammy and Grampy Miller still lived within visiting distance, and even though my schedule was busy, I tried to check in with them and visit as often as possible. I knew they weren't getting any younger with time, and that it wouldn't be long before they wouldn't be around.

Then one day I got that inevitable call. Grampy Miller had taken a fall, broken his hip, and was at the hospital. The doctors were honest with us. They said that an elderly gentleman at his age quite frequently didn't recover from a hip fracture. They often developed pneumonia from lying in bed while their hip mended, and that is exactly what happened to my grandfather. Before the hip had fully mended, he caught pneumonia and didn't have the strength to fight it off.

I was devastated. He had been such an active part of my childhood, and I knew I would miss him dearly. I worried about how Grammy would survive without him, and all the sorrow of losing him brought back the pain of losing Little Shay all those years ago. It was a difficult process to go through. However, it opened my eyes in a different way.

As I read his obituary in the local newspaper, it boasted of being married to my grandmother for close to sixty years. That was an amazing thought to me. It inspired me to want to set the same kind of record for myself, one that was steadfast and true, and proved how dependable a person I could be. Another thing that struck me in his obituary was that he only had two grandchildren – Kelli and me.

At this point in life, neither Kelli or I had gotten married or even thought about having kids. Kelli had dated a few guys, but none of them seriously. She was as hesitant about getting married as I was. However, if one of us didn't get married and start a family soon, there was no guarantee that Grammy Miller would ever have the opportunity to see one of her grandchildren walk down the aisle, or ever be allowed the privilege of holding a great-grandchild.

Yes, reading his obituary was truly a wake-up call for me. I knew just what I needed to do. Mandi and I needed to get married, and then I wanted to start a family. I had never been sure about it before, but it all seemed like the right thing to do now. It is what Grampy Miller would have wanted, and I didn't want my grandmother to miss out on her grandchild's wedding.

Within weeks of my grandfather's funeral, I had purchased a ring, proposed to Mandi, and she had accepted. We tackled our plans with fervor. We didn't want anything big and expensive. Informal and family-oriented was all we felt the need for. So, we used my dad's backyard, set up a flower-covered archway, and had a family barbeque. It was nothing elaborate, but it was good enough for us. Mandi's sister, Rachel, was the maid of honor. Rachel's daughter, Sarah, served as our flower girl. Of course, Ricky was my best man, and Rex was our ring bearer. How much more special could it be than that?!

Mandi had said "I do," the whole family had come to celebrate with us, Grammy Miller had the opportunity to see one of her grandchildren get married, and life was just about amazing. I was truly a happy person that day. I had a renewed sense of justice for life and couldn't wait to start a fresh life in paradise with the new Mrs. Jacob Miller. My life had been redeemed, and it would be smooth sailing from here on out.

CHAPTER 6
Flaws in Paradise

My childhood had been so tumultuous that I had promised myself I would be successful as an adult. I would make my life happen. When I married, it would be "'til death do we part." I would be the perfect husband, and bend over backwards, if that's what it took, to make my wife happy. Somehow, we would find a way to stay in love and have a thriving marriage.

When the kids came along, I would give them a "Rapini" style of life. We would be active, going places and doing things as a family. We would go to the beach on weekends during the summer, along with the bike riding and kite flying adventures. When winter came, I would find ways to keep my children entertained. I was determined my marriage and family would not fall apart like those of my childhood had.

We had a very good start to our marriage. Yes, we were successful in the eyes of the world. Mandi was working at a local hospital as a Licensed Practical Nurse, while I had found my own place in life working in the technical field of computers. We were making good money, had a nice apartment in a respectable neighborhood, owned a new car, and were just starting out life as a married couple. I'm sure there were people who would have envied us.

I didn't let pride well up inside of me, though. We had worked hard for what we had. Neither of us had ever shied away from hard work. It was a rewarding feeling to go to work each morning, fulfilling what we felt was our calling in life. Collecting a nice paycheck at the end of each week only made it a little better. Having struggled in my childhood years, I was truly thankful for every little blessing that came our way. I knew how challenging life could be, so these days of contentment were a time of renewal for me.

It was a feeling I cherished for the first few years of our independent lives together. But after a short time into married life, things began to change. The loving, kind, beautiful wife that I had married began to turn into a demanding nag. It was almost as though once she had that ring on her finger, she felt that she owned me and could tell me what to do all the time. While I may have been satisfied with the way things were going, she did not seem to share the same opinion.

The first few years of the "Honey Do List" didn't bother me too much. It made me feel needed and important. There were things she needed from me, and I was happy to do what I could to make her content. But after awhile, the list grew longer and longer, and if I failed to meet with her approval, she let me know that she was not happy about it. Keeping her smiling and cheerful started to become a real challenge, almost like having a second career. How could anyone be so needy all the time?

In spite of this, I began thinking seriously about a family. I felt like we had settled in well as a married couple, but I still wanted children. Amanda's sister, Rachel, had already produced two more children since Sarah, and I found that I really enjoyed being around them. It reminded me of the happy "Rapini years" that I had enjoyed so much as a child. It was the lifestyle I dreamed about having with a family of my own.

Not only that, but there was also the fact that Kelli still wasn't interested in marrying and settling down, and I wanted to be able to provide my dad with a grandchild, and a great-grandchild for Grammy Miller. Heaven knew she wasn't getting any younger, and who was to say how much longer she would be around. I also employed the thought that perhaps having a child would help Amanda feel fulfilled, maybe fill the void that was causing her to feel so unhappy.

But, when I approached her about the subject, it was definitely not met with approval. She let me know in no uncertain terms that she was not interested in bearing a child. I reminded her of the days when we had worked with the children after school at the Mentor's Program and how much she enjoyed them. To my surprise, she said she had only done that so she could spend some extra time with me.

Wow, that left me dumbfounded! I was honored that she had done it to spend time with me, but I thought she had done it for the kids like I had. My purpose for working in that program had been to do something productive in society, to help the next generation adjust to life, and walk away feeling rewarded as an added bonus. I had assumed those were feelings she had shared, too, but apparently I was wrong. Who, exactly, had I married? Maybe I didn't know her as well as I thought I did.

It was a subject I didn't dare approach again. She said Rex was the only child she would ever need. She clearly loved Rex. Sometimes, I thought she actually, liked Rex more than me. She would buy him toys, take him for ice cream, and always insisted that he go wherever we did. I enjoyed the affection she showered on him.

He was a good dog, and he deserved to be treated well. Yet, deep down inside, I still wanted a child of my own – one that would carry on the family name and someone to fill my shoes when I was gone. To me, life seemed meaningless if we couldn't pass life on to the next generation. But she seemed to have made up her mind, and there was no changing it.

So, I poured myself into my work instead. I told myself that lots of married couples didn't have kids, and we would just be happy without them. Rex would be our baby, although I don't know that my parents would have bragged about having a grand-dog. They would probably have much preferred a baby. And secretly, I hoped that Amanda would accidentally get pregnant and provide me with an offspring.

As time went on, I found I was good at keeping in touch with my dad. However, even though I had promised myself I would stay in touch with my mother, it just didn't seem to happen. She was too far away for a quick visit, and I never seemed to have enough time to reach out to her. Along with that, another side of Mandi emerged that I hadn't seen before, one that hindered the relationship with my mother.

Mandi had never said much about my mom while we were dating, but once we were married, she seemed to have plenty to say. She felt that my mother had abandoned me as a child. How could a mother just walk away from her child and not be there while they were growing up? She said if she had really cared about me, she would have made more of an effort to be there. She would have come for visits, or made the drive over to attend school events and milestones.

At first, I was quick to defend my mother. I knew it was a long drive for her, and she was working full-time while trying to raise Ricky and Nicole. I knew she had a full schedule, and while I had missed having her in my teenage years, I had always tried to understand her position. But Amanda didn't see it that way. She said it is a mother's responsibility to always be there for their child, and was quick to point out how supportive her mother had been.

After her repeated arguments through the years, I began to resent my mother for having left me. It would have been just as easy for her to reach out to me as it was for me to reach out to her. And, yet she hadn't, so maybe Mandi was right. Maybe my mother had abandoned me, just walked away and left me in the care of my father because she didn't have time for me. Or, maybe she just didn't like me.

Whatever the case, I failed to nurture my relationship with my mother. I found the years drifting by without communicating with her. She tried several times reaching out to me, but I ignored her efforts. The resentment of having been left behind as a child was hard to overcome. Rather than addressing the problem and dealing with my feelings, I suppressed them and let the bitterness build. Mandi was right. My mother had abandoned me as a child and should have made more of an effort to be there for me.

As usual, I let work be my counselor. Keeping myself busy kept my mind occupied. I had Mandi and Rex as my family now. Even though it seemed they were all I would ever have, I was determined that I would be happy and satisfied with my blessings. I was resilient and had made it this far in life. We would be happy and make life work for us. It would frequently take a beer or two after work to put a smile on my face, but I told myself that was okay. Other people drink, too, and they seemed to do okay in life. So, it was all good for me.

Until the day when it wasn't. It came on gradually, as most problems in life do. They have a way of sneaking up on you, just a little ache here or there, and you don't realize how big a problem you have brewing inside of you. However, those little aches finally developed into pain that was hard to ignore. I knew I had put on some pounds and hadn't necessarily been eating properly. I was probably consuming more alcohol than I ought to, and felt I just needed some guidance regarding how to correct my problem. So, I scheduled an appointment with my doctor, thinking maybe I just needed to make some dietary changes.

I expected a simple solution, but what I got was a stunning diagnosis. I had pancreatitis! It was a painful, debilitating illness that had no easy cure. I didn't know what to do for it, but I can tell you what it did to me. It frequently left me curled up in a ball on the floor, writhing with pain. And when I wasn't in pain, I was in the bathroom. Diarrhea became a commonplace thing for me. I hardly dared to go out in public anymore, because it wasn't always easy to find a bathroom. And, when I needed one, I needed it fast!

The pancreatitis put me into a tailspin that was hard to recover from. My boss was not happy with the amount of time I was spending in the bathroom. He called me into the office and quite frankly told me that he wasn't paying me to sit in the restroom all day. I tried to explain that it was a medical condition I couldn't help for now, and that I hoped it was a temporary problem until I could learn to manage it.

I had been there long enough that he should have known I was a good worker. But he was not sympathetic and understanding about my situation. He told me to stay out of the bathroom, or use the main entrance to make my exit.

I tried desperately to use the bathroom as infrequently as possible, but it was useless. I couldn't control the demands of my body. When it said to go, I had to go, or I would regret it. Then the inevitable happened. One day my boss called me into the office, told me to pack up my belongings, and leave.

I was stunned. I thought my work ethics would have been enough to carry me through, and that he would have been understanding enough to work with me. However, he clearly didn't care about my situation. I had failed to meet with his expectations, so now I was fired. My argument that with time I would be able to manage the problem only fell on deaf ears. He remained firm. There was the door, and please use it.

I didn't dare go home to face Amanda. We had developed a lifestyle that she was happy with, and there was no way we could continue this standard of living on a single income. Plus, it was humiliating to be fired from a job I loved so much, and over such a personal and embarrassing issue.

Not daring to go home, I hopped onto the highway and started driving. My mind was going faster than what I could keep up with, and I had no idea where I was going. I was over an hour and a half away from home when I came to my senses and realized things were out-of-whack.

Something had to change in my life. That suddenly became very clear to me. I couldn't make Amanda happy when I was working, and it certainly wasn't going to improve now. I had failed to maintain a relationship with my mother, like I had promised I would, and now the feelings of anger and bitterness over being abandoned were stronger than ever.

Any sense of loss always brought up the painful memories of losing Little Shay and my Rapini family. And now, added to all the other emotional baggage, was my physical condition. My body dictated my every move and had caused me to become unemployed, leaving me with no career and little chance of finding another job in my condition.

Finally, in a state of utter defeat, I turned the car around and went home to face my wife. I sobbed uncontrollably on the couch, shedding tears of defeat and failure, as I shared my heartache with Amanda. I couldn't seem to pull myself together, so we both decided maybe I needed to seek some professional help. We went to a local mental health facility, where I was admitted to an overnight program. I was relieved at the thought of finally getting some help to address the issues of my past and give me a brighter outlook for the future.

Life had always presented me with one challenge after another, and it didn't seem anxious to change now. I had high hopes of conquering the bundled up mess that I had become, but I had lost my insurance coverage when I lost my job. I was more than welcome to stay, they told me, and they would love to help me with my needs and concerns. However, it would have to be treated as a self pay situation, and I would be responsible for all the financial aspects. This they told the man who had just lost his job and wasn't sure how to make ends meet on a single income.

As much as I needed this help, I knew I couldn't afford the expense of the program. So, the bundled up mess that I had become, packed what few belongings I had brought with me, and headed home. My room number during my brief stay had been 4213, so I had those numbers tattooed on the fingers of my right hand. I thought maybe if I had something I could physically look at, it would remind me to hold myself together and that I had what it took to get through this thing called life.

I decided not to give up and applied for another job. I was quickly hired, and my hope was restored. However, it wasn't long before I lost that job, too, due to the complications of my medical condition. The next several months became a series of getting hired and fired. I went through about four more jobs before I finally had to accept the fact that I was no longer a desirable employee. I spent too much time in the bathroom, and no employer was going to pay me to do that.

Maybe I could find a way to work from home. Maybe I could start my own computer business, set up a website and advertise online to generate some income. I still had Mandi and Rex, and we would just have to find a way to get through this together. Hopefully, my physical problems would resolve, and I could get back to living again.

Maybe if I ate the right foods, found some over-the-counter medications that would help, and started an exercise program, the pain would go away. And definitely try to avoid any alcoholic beverages. That's what had started the problem to begin with, along with medications I had taken as a teenager to control my acne. But the alcohol consumption was harder to gain control of than I expected. Even though I knew it complicated my physical problems, it gave me the emotional release I needed.

I tried to stay positive and frequently reminded myself that I was resilient. I had been through a lot in my lifetime, and I would get through this, too. With more free time on my hands, I could do some research on this illness and try to find ways to help myself.

This was my life, and I was going to make it work. It's what I had told myself many times in the past. I couldn't control my childhood, but adulthood was in my own hands. I would improve the quality of my life, one way or another. Now, I just had to find a way to convince my body to cooperate with my plans.

CHAPTER 7
Bittersweet Encounters

I had held such high hopes for my life as an adult. Mandi and I had spent hours lying under the stars in my father's backyard, planning our future together and talking about how our lives would go. Yet, here I was, facing the fact that there was a lot in my life that I had no control over. The biggest issue was my health. There was no direct cure and, as hard as I tried, I couldn't seem to find a way to successfully manage the pain. It consumed me and dictated my actions from the moment I woke up until I finally crawled into bed at night, in a state of total defeat.

It seemed the things I could control in my life were gradually slipping through my fingers like beach sand, one grain at a time. I couldn't make my wife happy. I had lost my job. We were having tremendous financial problems. I had lost contact with my mother, whom I had hoped would be a source of support and strength for me. My body was a mess, to the point where I had resorted to substance abuse just to make it through the day. I had told myself I would stop drinking, but found I relied on alcohol to sedate myself. I also found I was taking too many of my pain pills on a daily basis, just to try to control the pain level.

The drinking and drugging left me feeling completely defeated. How had it ever come to this? I had always shunned those who did drugs and needed to rely on external substances to make it through the day, and now I was one of them. I needed the alcohol to numb me and found myself abusing my own medications, just as a means of survival. And when I had emptied the bottle of pain pills before it was time for a refill, well, then I found myself in serious trouble. Arguing with my doctors and pharmacists got me nowhere, except frustrated, still in pain, and now with a bad reputation. I was not an aggressive person, but they just didn't understand my pain. They probably considered me to be a drug addict, like some of their other patients, only seeking to gain more medications for the purpose of abuse.

But my pain was real. It was incredibly real. I sometimes wished

I could just pass out so I wouldn't have to feel it anymore. The only thing that gave me real joy at that point in my life was Rex. He was always beside me, trying to cheer me up, especially when I felt I could take no more. If I was lying on the floor in a ball of agony and defeat, he was laying beside me, almost as if to say, "I'm here for you, buddy. I don't know how to help you, but I am right here if you need me." He was definitely my best friend and more devoted than my wife.

I think Amanda was in agreement with the doctors, thinking that I was just looking for more medication. I often wished that they could feel my pain, so they would know how real it was. She tried to control my prescription medications and kept them locked up. Every morning, she would leave me the daily allotment on the table, along with a long list of things she expected me to do while she was at work. Since she was supporting us, she expected that I would take care of all the household tasks while she was away. And Heaven help us if I failed to complete the list.

My favorite part of the daily list was where she allowed time for me to take Rex to the park for a walk. Most of the time, I felt guilty if I left the house. It seemed the least I could do was to stay home and clean, keeping the dishes and laundry done and the apartment tidy. But, taking Rex for a walk was acceptable in her eyes. It was a legitimate reason for me to be outdoors and not stuck inside cleaning all day. And Rex enjoyed it as much as I did.

Then one day while we were walking in the park, something totally unexpected happened. I noticed Jacki there with some children. I hadn't seen her since high school, but I would have recognized her anywhere. The rapid beating of my heart only confirmed that it was really her. But would she remember me? Had she even noticed me all those years ago when we went to school together? Maybe she hadn't even known I existed.

For the first couple of encounters, I just observed her from a distance. I still had fears of loss and abandonment, and I was afraid if I approached her, she wouldn't even remember that we had gone to school together. Staying away was better than taking a chance at another opportunity to be rejected. But every time she was there, I threw Rex's ball a little closer to the swings, where she was playing with her kids.

Then one day, she looked my way. I expected her to just glance away, but she didn't. She seemed to focus on my face for a moment, and then a smile of recognition formed on hers.

"Hey, aren't you Jacob Miller?" she smiled at me. "Didn't we go to school together?"

Wow, she did know who I was, and she had recognized me even

after so many years apart! I was dumbfounded and almost tongue-tied when I tried to answer her. She still gave me butterflies and made me feel like I was back in school, facing my very first crush.

That first face-to-face encounter turned into a daily routine. Every morning when I took Rex to the park after that, she always seemed to be there. I found my daily trip to the park to be much more enjoyable, not just because I could get out of the house and spend some time with Rex, but because Jacki always seemed to be waiting for me, and actually seemed to enjoy my company.

Then one day, she invited me to her place for coffee. Something inside of me said it wasn't a smart move, but I couldn't help myself. I had always been fascinated by Jacki, and she was so kind to me. She seemed to want to spend time with me and was interested in my life, unlike my wife. Mandi made me feel like I was nothing more than a burden to her, just someone she had to take care of because he couldn't take care of himself. When I was with Amanda, I felt like I was just her pawn, waiting for her to make the next move in her game of control. But Jacki made me feel like a man again.

So even though instinct said to stay away, I went to Jacki's apart-ment for a visit. It was just for a cup of coffee initially, but it didn't take long before Jacki and I found ourselves involved in a physical relationship. And to add to the problem, she got me into smoking pot. It helped me to relax and forget my problems for awhile, but Mandi would have been furious if she found out. Plus, what would my family think?

I somehow managed to keep my affair with Jacki a secret from Amanda for quite some time. However, I was an emotional mess. Even though I had been through a bit of a tumultuous childhood, I was raised knowing right from wrong, and I knew what I was doing was terribly wrong. I was a married man, and she was a married woman. We had no right to be together. And while I was snuggling with Jacki, my wife was working hard to support us and keep a roof over our heads.

My head and heart were in a constant battle. My head was always quick to remind me of the errors of my ways, but my heart was happy. It soared when I was with Jacki. She gave my life an element of joy that I hadn't felt for a very long time. She made me feel loved and wanted. My marriage had been missing that touch ever since I had lost my job and it had become Amanda's role to support us. I knew someday it would all come to a climax and Amanda would find out, but I couldn't stop the emo-tions I felt for Jacki. I decided I was in it for the duration, however long it might last.

I tried to be loving and kind to Amanda so she wouldn't suspect anything. If she knew I was having an affair, she might get mad and kick me out. And where could a man in my condition go? No one would want to take in a deadbeat like me, someone who couldn't even work to support his family. My body was still in such a state of chaos that working was currently not an option.

****

During this time frame, I had another surprise encounter. Mandi and I were at the store shopping when we bumped into one of my Rapini stepsiblings. We were preparing for a Fourth of July celebration, and shopping in the grocery store for supplies, when I turned the corner at the end of the aisle and came face-to-face with Mariah. I hadn't seen her since the day we stood in the yard together and watched my mom and Paul drive off to their new life without us.

Even though it had been quite some time, we recognized each other instantly.

"Jakie, Jr.!" she exclaimed, reaching out to give me a quick hug. "You are just a little bit bigger than you were the last time I saw you."

We laughed together and completely forgot about grocery shopping. We talked for the next twenty minutes or so. I introduced her to Amanda and told her how I hadn't seen mom and Kelli much. They were just too far away, and life was too busy to get together. I didn't tell her my wife had convinced me that my mother had deserted me.

Mariah confessed that she had also tried to keep in touch with dad, but she had trouble finding time to visit as well. Then she said her brothers and her were having a family barbeque tomorrow to celebrate the holiday. She said she was sure Mason and "Big Jake" would love to see me.

It had been such a long time since I had seen any of them, so Mandi and I quickly agreed to stop by the next day. I was so excited at having seen her, and couldn't wait to see my two stepbrothers that I hadn't seen for years. I was almost like a kid on Christmas Eve that night, and had a hard time sleeping.

The barbeque was going to be at Mariah's mother's house, so the next day we headed that way, arriving shortly before lunch time. There was a hearty round of greetings, with hugs between the four of us – Mason, Big Jake, Mariah, and Little Jake. It was a jovial reunion. We were so happy to be together again, and it was like we had just seen each other yesterday.

We sat around the picnic table in their backyard and caught up on lost time. They had all settled locally, staying close to their mother. Occasionally they had made it over to visit Paul and my mom, but as with me, life was too busy to visit as often as they wanted. There was some comfort in knowing that I wasn't the only one who had lost touch with the wonderful relationships we had had as a family.

Sitting there visiting together made us wonder why we hadn't made the effort to connect sooner. It was like old times, like we had never been apart from each other. The camaraderie and fondness we had held for each other when we were a family was still there. We laughed and joked like we had in our childhood.

I hadn't felt this blessed in a very long time, and I think they enjoyed our time together as much as I did. We reminisced about childhood events, laughing about the night we mounted our spaghetti dinner on the dining room wall, talking about all our family trips to the lake, and the day Little Shay acquired her nickname. At the mention of Shay, our laughter quickly ceased and the joviality faded. She had been gone for years, yet the pain of losing her was still as real as if it had happened just yesterday. She had been such a happy part of our family, and was still deeply missed by all of us.

After a brief moment of silence, Mariah spoke up and said, "She was quite a kid." She smiled at her memory, and we all nodded and chorused in agreement that she truly was a memorable child.

The afternoon flew by, and I was soaring internally at having spent such an enjoyable day with my long lost siblings. I anticipated leaving on a high note and reveling in the joy that I was feeling when a man I didn't recognize stumbled out the door of the house. My stepsibings glanced his way, and I noticed they all immediately acquired an expression of concern.

His wayward steps led him directly to our gathering. As he gazed around our group, his unfriendly stare settled on me.

"Who do we have here?" he demanded gruffly.

Big Jake quickly spoke up and explained that I was Little Jake that used to be an active part of their family.

"Oh," he nodded his head in recognition, "I've heard about you. You're the one they used to call Jakie, Jr."

I smiled, pleased that my stepsiblings had shared my reputation with him. They must have said something about me for him to know who I was. But he was quick to shoot down my moment of glory.

"Jakie, Jr!" he scoffed. "You ain't no Jakie, Jr. You never were and you never will be. This family only needs one Jacob, and he's sitting right here." He pointed to Big Jake, who sat at the table looking very uncomfortable.

Mariah was quick to come to my defense. "Stop it, Ron!" she insisted. "Jakie is here as our guest. I invited him, and you have no right to be so rude!"

I looked at Amanda, and she nodded toward the car, indicating that we should probably leave. I had had such a wonderful afternoon and didn't want to leave on a sour note, but I clearly didn't want to stay and suffer anymore abuse at the hands of this stranger.

"I think we will head home now," I said, as Amanda and I stood and gathered our belongings together.

"No, Jakie, you don't have to leave," Mason spoke up. "If anyone needs to go, it's Ron. He has had too much to drink, and he needs to go sober up."

But the damage was already done. For whatever he held against me, he had clearly voiced his disapproval, and the bitter words had cut deep. I diplomatically told them that it was alright, Amanda and I really needed to head home anyway. I thanked them for a wonderful afternoon and gave them all a round of hugs.

As we walked toward the car, Ron was still on a rampage. "Good riddance, Jakie, Jr!" he called to my departing back. "The Rapini family has functioned just fine without you, and they will continue to do so."

My stepsiblings all quickly told him to shut his mouth, but the painful words struck me hard, almost as though someone was throwing sharp darts at my back. And, unfortunately, they were making contact every time.

Mariah walked to our car with us, apologizing profusely all the way. She explained that Ron was her mother's new boyfriend, and that he was typically a nice guy. However, when he drinks, he could become a mean drunk.

"What does he have against me?" I asked her.

She shrugged her shoulders and said she didn't really know. "I think just that you are a part of our past, and that is something he can't control. He wants to be the father of our family, with just us and no reminders that we had successfully existed without him. That apparently is what you are to him – a reminder that there was a time when we had a life, and we didn't need him. And it was a happy life, too, I might add!"

She did all she could to make up for the pain that he had caused, gave me one more hug before I got into the car, and told me to keep in touch. Even though I knew that my Rapini siblings did not share the sentiment of the words Ron had uttered, the sting of those bitter words hung heavy in my head and heart. They played over and over in my head as I drove down the road, words of hatred that kept bouncing around inside of me, causing bruises as they did.

They finally upset me so much, that I pulled the car over and asked Mandi to drive home. My whole being was so perplexed I couldn't even focus on the road and didn't want to pass my heartache on to some innocent, unsuspecting motorist out enjoying the holiday. It was better to let someone else, who was more in control of their faculties, take the wheel and guide us safely home. Then I could just focus on overcoming the pain that I was feeling, which wasn't just physical anymore. My aching body was now accompanied by a very troubled soul.

CHAPTER 8
Paradise Gone

The pain of the encounter with my Rapini family burned inside of me for days. Not just days, actually, but it went on for weeks. I didn't have enough to do to keep myself occupied so I could stop thinking about it. Mandi was sympathetic for a day or two. She definitely felt bad about what Ron had said. However, after a few days of seeing me mope around, she regained her tough shell and told me to get over it. She said I couldn't pout about it forever. I needed to grow up and move on.

The only thing that got me through those days was my daily visits with Jacki. All the feelings of abandonment and rejection from my past seemed to fade away when she wrapped her arms around me. She was the only person that really made me feel loved and wanted in life. Her words of sympathy seemed real and sincere. Night times were especially hard, though. Night after night of lying beside my cold-hearted wife only made me long more for Jacki. I wished desperately that she could be the one snuggling up to me at night, the one I could share my hopes, dreams, and heartaches with. It seemed the further apart Amanda and I drifted, the closer Jacki and I grew.

When I would roll over in despair and sigh at my situation, Rex would always be there beside the bed to comfort me. He seemed to understand the pain I was feeling, whether I was in physical pain or emotional pain. He would poke my arm with his cold, wet nose until I reached out to pet him. No matter what it was that I was facing, Rex was always there for me. He was definitely a devoted friend.

****

I made two critical errors at this point in my life. One was that I went to my dad's house and got my guns. He had bought me a hunting rifle and a pistol while I was still living at home to use when we went hunting, and I had left them there when I moved out. There didn't seem to be any reason to bring them with me. They were safe at his house, and I could go there to get them if I wanted to go hunting.

However, the bitter words Ron had thrown at me left me feeling very insecure. Added to that was the fact that a convicted murderer had moved into our neighborhood, and I felt the need to protect Amanda and myself. I was trained to use a gun, but hoped I would never have to do so. If this man ever posed a threat to us, I could simply make him aware that I had a gun, and that I was very capable of using it. I had become a very good marksman and quite capable of hitting my target. Maybe sharing that knowledge with him would be enough to keep him away, if it ever came to that. I hoped and prayed that it wouldn't, but I kept my rifle in the apartment and the pistol in a compartment of the car for security.

My other error was in inviting Jacki over to my place one day while Amanda was at work. I don't really even know why I did it. We had always met at her place, and the arrangement had worked well. Maybe I just wanted her to see a part of my world and know where I lived. But on that particular day when we met at the park, she happened to be alone. Her kids had gone to visit some friends, and my place was closer than hers.

Everything might have turned out okay, but it was a little chilly that morning when we met. After staying at my place for a couple of hours, the day had warmed considerably, and she no longer needed her jacket. So, she forgot it when she left, leaving it hanging on the coat rack in my apartment. After she was gone, I quickly cleaned up, trying to make sure everything was in its place and there was no evidence of her visit. But I didn't notice the jacket hanging on the rack until Amanda got home and went to hang her coat up. And, of course, she immediately noticed the unfamiliar jacket.

Prior to this incident, my fights with Amanda had always been verbal. We had yelled and hollered at each other, and she frequently called me names. After finding Jacki's coat in our apartment, though, Amanda became physically aggressive. As if the pain from my condition hadn't been enough to deal with, now I had the wrath of Amanda to add to it. She would beat on me, punching, kicking, slapping, or whatever happened to strike her fancy at the moment, making my pain even worse. One time she twisted my arm up behind my back and sprained it. I couldn't go to the doctor and tell them my wife had done it, so I just nursed it until it healed on its own. I told myself I deserved this pain. I had brought this problem on myself by being unfaithful to my wife, so the pain was a reminder of my shortcomings and failures as a husband.

I never fought back against Amanda. I could easily understand her frustration. She was working so hard to support us, while I was doing nothing to help with our financial situation and having an affair on the side. The work issue was not my fault. I wanted to work and had acquired multiple jobs throughout the last couple of years, but none of them had lasted. I looked healthy on the outside, but most employers didn't understand what was brewing inside of me and wouldn't tolerate my frequent trips to the restroom. Some jobs lasted a couple of months, while others lasted only a few days.

I desperately wanted to work and earn an income to help support our household, but it seemed the only option was to work remotely from the bathroom. It was a real blow to my ego, which was one of the reasons why I continued my affair with Jacki. It was the only thing that made me feel like a man, and gave me meaning and purpose in life. But now, Amanda had found out about the affair and life had only become more complicated. But as violent as she became, I always walked away. I had been taught to treat woman with respect, plus it was my nature to run from confrontation anyway. When it came to "fight or flight," I was usually flapping my wings and ready for take off!

****

I knew things needed to change, but I continued to see Jacki secretly while Amanda continued with the demands that I end the affair. My head and heart fought each other continuously. I knew she was right. I had to confront Jacki and tell her it was over. It was the right thing to do. I had married Amanda for better or worse, until death do we part. It was one of the things I had admired so much about Grampy Miller. He had been faithful and true all of his life, and I wanted to be like him. He would never have gotten himself into a situation like this.

Thinking about my Miller grandparents filled me with a desire to go visit Grammy Miller. I hadn't seen her for awhile and wondered how she was doing. I told myself that she wasn't getting any younger, and I should spend some time with her while I could. Plus, maybe a chat with her would give me the courage to do what I needed to do. Perhaps a reminder of how two people could remain devoted to each other would make me want to become a better husband and recommit myself to my wife.

However, it was like life itself read my thoughts and decided to deal another blow. Before I had a chance to go see her, Grammy Miller had a stroke and passed away. Just like that, and she was gone. I should have gone to see her sooner; I shouldn't have let life get in the way and keep me from spending time with her. I hadn't been to see her for months, and now I would never have the opportunity again. Grammy Miller was gone. My rock, my strength, the person who had provided me with so much guidance throughout my childhood, and now she was no more.

We attended her funeral a few days later. As I stood beside her freshly dug grave, it became clear to me what I needed to do. I had married Mandi for life, and Grammy Miller would want me to stand by my wife. It's what Grammy and Grampy Miller had done for close to sixty years, and they were the example I wanted to follow. It definitely wasn't the relationship I wanted at this time in my life, but maybe things would get better. Maybe if I did the right thing, life would smile on me and give me another chance. Perhaps my body would heal, I could get a steady job to help support us, Mandi would settle down, and we would be happy again. It seemed like a tall order, but taking the first step by doing the right thing might just start us down the road to reconciliation and recovery.

****

The next day, I met Jacki at the park like usual. But instead of going to her house for a visit, I told her that we were finished. I was staying with Mandi, so I wouldn't be able to see her anymore. I expected her to cry, plead with me to stay, beg me not to go. We had had such a wonderful relationship together, and I thought our breaking up would be devastating to her.

She did none of those, though. She remained calm, looking me in the eye, and simply said, "Yeah, you're right. It's for the best. We are both married and shouldn't have had an affair to begin with."

All of what she said was true. We were both married to other people, and it was for the best that we stay true to our partners. And yes, we should never have let it go as far as it had. But the way she said it caught me by surprise. She sounded almost cold, detached, emotionless, like all that we had been through together just didn't matter.

My emotions were all tangled up inside of me. I had been so nervous about confronting her, but now I was hurt, almost feeling ashamed for having loved her so much. Those old feelings of abandonment and rejection were quick to resurface. How could she turn her back on all that we had shared together so easily and not feel like fighting for me? Not that it really mattered. As far as I was concerned, the affair was over. But I wanted to know that I was important to her, that she would miss our time together, and that wasn't quite the reaction I was getting from her, or the response that I had expected.

After Jacki's nonchalant dismissal of our affair, I felt an incredible vacuum in my life. My mom had come to Grammy Miller's funeral, of course, and it made me realize how much I had missed her. She had been quick to reach out and give me a hug, showing that she did love me and was glad to see me. Now that Grammy Miller wasn't around to talk to any-more, I decided to pick up my phone the next day and call my mother.

I wasn't sure what to expect, but she truly sounded concerned about what I was going through. I told her all about my affair with Jacki, how Amanda had been cruel, spiteful, and physically aggressive toward me, and how I felt useless and full of despair. I wasn't sure I could go on living without Jacki's interaction. She had been my motivation to get out of bed in the morning. Without her in my life, Rex was the only thing that brought me happiness.

My emotions boiled out of me in that conversation, and I soon found myself sobbing into my cell phone. I poured out my heart to my mother, shared my shortcomings with her, and told her all of my frustra-tions in life. No matter how hard I tried, I just couldn't seem to get a break. I wanted a fresh start, but had no idea how to do that. How had life come to this point? I thought I was resilient and could handle anything that came my way, but I was totally overwhelmed.

My mom was so sympathetic and kind. It made me wish I had called her a long time ago. She suggested that I come to stay with her for awhile. Maybe getting away for a bit would help me to clear my head and figure out what to do next. It sounded like such a good plan talking to her about it, but when I presented my idea to Amanda later that day, she hit the roof.

"Why are you talking to your mom?" she demanded. "She aban-doned you! She wasn't there for you in your teenage years, and left you without a mother when you needed her the most. Do you really think she's going to rescue you now?!"

Her words were mean and harsh. They stung like I had just stum-bled into a hive of angry bees. How did she even know my mother? She had only met her a couple of times. Her interactions with my mom were limited and only scratched the surface. I had known her all my life, even if I hadn't lived with her. Amanda had no right to be so judgmental. Plus, I didn't know if my mother had the answer, but I knew she cared about me and the mess that had become my life. She seemed more willing to help me than my wife did. Amanda's anger lately ran deep, and she cut me down at every opportunity.

I was torn over what to do. My mom's suggestion seemed so reasonable. It made sense. I needed a new start. But Amanda would never let me take Rex with me. I knew that without even asking. I had just lost Jacki, and I couldn't bear to lose Rex, too. So the next day, I called my mom and thanked her for the suggestion, but I would stay with Amanda and try to make it work. She reassured me that it was an open offer and she was there if I needed her. She would be thinking about me, praying for me, and that I was welcome to call any time I needed to talk.

I hung up the phone with a sense of despair. I knew I had a challenging walk ahead of me, but I hoped desperately that the tables would soon take a turn. I had tolerated enough loss and shortcomings in life, and it seemed that fate had to give me a break. I just needed to be strong, to persevere, and someday soon, maybe things would get better. My body would just have to heal so, I could get a job. That was the key factor. The lack of money was what bothered my wife the most, so I would just keep trying until I found a job I could keep, one I could do from home, or a way to successfully manage the symptoms of my illness. I had to make Grammy and Grampy Miller proud of me, and my parents as well. I would pull myself up by the boot straps and move forward, one way or another.

I can do this, I told myself over and over. But did I really believe it? With all that was going on in my life, was it even possible to overcome everything and gain the upper hand? Did I rule my life, or had it taken control of me?

CHAPTER 9
The Fateful Day

So many emotions were all tangled up inside me, and I didn't know how to get them straightened out. I tried to be strong and take control of my life. Yet, it seemed that before I had a chance to wrestle one problem to the mat, another one would pop up and only complicate the twisted mess further.

The pep talks I had been giving myself were growing harder and harder to believe. I wanted to trust my ability to manage the things that were happening in my life, but it wasn't all up to me. I needed some help from my wife. She had to want to try, too. And a little cooperation from my body would have been good as well.

The bottom line was that I was exhausted with life. I was tired from struggling to manage my illness. I was frustrated with trying to make ends meet on a single income, and not being able to help my wife out with the finances. I was sick of trying to make my wife happy, and always falling short of that goal. And, quite frankly, I was tired of trying to make myself happy. Life had turned out to be a lot more work than I had ever expected, and I just didn't know what to do about it. Nor did I know if I even wanted to try anymore.

I knew the solution that made the most sense was to walk away from the life I was living, go stay with my mom, get some psychiatric help, and start over again. But I wasn't sure I wanted to do that. With all we had been through, I did still love Mandi. And I think, in her own way, she loved me, too. I hoped we could just find a way to gain control of this situation and get back to the way we used to be. Why couldn't she accept that staying with my mother would only be temporary?

Yet, I knew if I left, Amanda would probably make my life miserable. She would see it as a failure or think I was running away from her. She might decide I was leaving her for Jacki, or going to find someone new. I was convinced that nothing I said could change her mind, and that somehow she would make me pay for leaving. As angry as she sometimes was, my departure would probably trigger her to throw all of my belongings away, destroy them, or sell them to get what she could for them. The Jacob Miller I had been all of my life would probably cease to exist.

In a way, that was a pleasing thought. My life had been challenging, for sure, and the thought of starting over and trying to become the person I wanted to be was a reassuring one. But did I have that kind of courage? That was a major step, and I doubted that there would be any turning back once I made it.

Then one day, Amanda made the decision for me. She came home from work in an exceptionally pleasant mood, treating me kindly and asking how my day went. Most days, she walked through the door with disgust in her eyes, acting like the very sight of me was repulsive and almost more than she could tolerate. Her pleasant attitude that day caught me by surprise.

After dinner, she asked me to run to the store and get some milk and bread. She gave me extra money and told me to treat myself to something I wanted. Maybe get a pack of cigarettes, some soda, or even a case of beer if I wanted. Money had been an issue for a very long time, and her sudden generosity left me almost speechless. Usually, I had to beg for money for the things I wanted, or even needed, for that matter.

As I drove to the store, I felt happy. It was a feeling I hadn't felt since breaking up with Jacki. But Mandi seemed to be her cheerful old self, and that made me feel good inside. I had told her about my breakup with Jacki, so maybe she had accepted it and was ready to move on. Maybe we had turned the corner and things were going to start to improve.

I knew things could get better, but I hadn't been sure that Mandi believed it or even wanted to make our relationship work. But to see her smile and be kind again made me realize maybe we did have a chance at saving our marriage.

When I returned from the store, I immediately noticed something was different. Rex always met me at the door. We had become almost inseparable since I had stopped working and spent so much time at home. I set my bags on the table and called out to him, but he didn't respond. I whistled a few times, but still nothing.

I went into the living room and asked Mandi where Rex was hiding. She appeared to be wrapped up in something on TV and at first didn't respond to me. Then she turned my way, smiled sweetly, and said, "I gave him away. My sister wanted a dog for her kids, and I thought Rex would fit nicely into their family."

At first, I thought she was joking. She wouldn't just give Rex away.

He was a part of our family, and I thought she loved him as much as I did. So I questioned her further.

"You're joking, right?" I asked.

She looked casually over at me and replied that it was no joke. We couldn't afford a dog anyway. Funds had been very tight, so it just didn't make sense to support a dog when we were struggling to take care of ourselves.

To say I was angry would be the understatement of the year. I was livid! Almost insanely angry! How could she just give my dog away like that, as though he wasn't a part of this family and he didn't matter? Like he was nothing more than an expensive burden that we couldn't afford? Without Jacki in my life, he had been my only reason for crawling out of bed in the morning. If they were both gone, then what was the point in even living?

I went from room to room searching for him, hoping that this was just some kind of sick joke. But finally, I had to accept the truth. Rex was gone. She had really given him away and my buddy was no longer here. My first thought was to go after him and take him back, but then a vision of Sarah's distraught face came to mind. I knew she loved Rex, too, and if I tried taking him back, she would probably hate me and think I was evil.

Sleep was elusive that night. I didn't even try to go to bed. For one thing, I didn't want to sleep in the same bed as my wife. She had done some irritating things in the past, but she had never been this mean and spiteful. I felt like my life was over. There was no point of even trying anymore. I spent the night sitting on the couch, staring at the television. I have no recollection of what I even watched. My mind was too occupied to take in any new information.

The next morning, Amanda left for work as usual, without even so much as a farewell greeting. I didn't care. I didn't feel like working on our relationship anymore. She had burned the last bridge, and now I felt like I was alone on an isolated island. I knew I needed to talk to someone who cared, so I picked up the phone and called my mother. I sobbed uncontrollably as I told her about Amanda's evil deed. She encouraged me to just pack my bags and head her way. She had a spare room and would get it ready for me.

I was a ticking time bomb. My mom knew it, and I did, too. It was like I had an unexploded hand grenade inside me. The pin was about to drop out, and I knew I would be unable to stop the eruption of powerful explosives nestled deep inside should that happen. The destruction of what might possibly come about could be devastating, and it would probably affect more than just me. I had to find a way to get control of what was brewing inside.

I reassured my mom that I would start packing, but then I made a fateful mistake. I told her I had something to do before heading her way, but would be there soon. After hanging up the phone, I pointed myself in the direction of the park where I used to take Rex. My hope was that I would bump into Jacki.

I just wanted to let her know I was leaving town for awhile. Not that it really mattered anymore. Our relationship was over, but I didn't want her to think I had disappeared for good. I wanted her to know that I was going to get some help to try to pull my life back together, and that I would be back someday soon. When I did come back, hopefully I would be in better shape, just incase she ever needed a friend to talk to. Plus, I secretly wondered if she was missing me yet.

Jacki was there, as I had hoped she would be, but yet I wasn't sure I should approach her. She seemed happy with her kids, and I didn't want to upset her. Plus, as much of a mess as I was inside, I knew I would probably turn into a blubbering idiot and sob my eyes out. However, she spotted me and noticed I was alone.

"Where's Rex?" she called over to me.

That was all it took. A concerned voice that wanted to know what had happened to my dog. I dropped down on the bench located beside me, the one we had chatted on day after day while the kids had played. But this time, I sat in a state of total defeat. As many happy times as we had shared sitting on that bench, they couldn't lift my spirits today. She could see that something was wrong and quickly came over to join me.

I hung my head and poured out my heart to her. I told her how Amanda had given Rex away out of spite, just as a means of punishing me. I said that I felt there was nothing left to live for without her or Rex in my life.

Jacki was truly concerned. She rubbed my back as I sobbed, tried to convince me that I was strong, and told me that I would get through this. But I didn't know if I agreed with her. I had never felt so defeated in my whole life, and there just didn't seem to be any point in trying any more. I couldn't save my marriage if my wife wasn't willing to work with me. A relationship took two, and I felt like I was the only one interested in reviving ours.

Jacki called to a friend and asked her to keep an eye on the kids for a few minutes. Then she took me by the hand and said, "Come with me."

She brought me to her house, gave me a joint, and told me to smoke it to calm myself down. Afterwards, we sat on her porch and talked for awhile. I told her of my plans to go spend time with my mother and get some psychiatric help. She agreed that it was probably a good idea. Her pep talk was what I needed. If only Amanda could have been as supportive and given me encouragement like that. Things could be so different.

After we had talked for awhile, Jacki said she needed to go back to the park to get her kids. I told her that I didn't know when I would be back or how long this would take, but I would miss her and the times we had spent together. As a means of thanking her for the support, I gave her a big hug. She pulled back and looked at me. I'm sure the sorrow was written plainly on my face as I fought hard to hold back the tears.

"Look at me," she said. She lifted my chin until our eyes met, and then said, "You are a good man, Jacob Miller. You have just run into a very difficult time in your life, but you will get through this. Just know that even though we won't be together, I will be thinking of you and cheering for you. Think of me as your own private cheerleader who believes in your ability to win this game."

I could picture her as a cheerleader back in school all those years ago, and the thought brought a smile to my face. As I gazed into her eyes, I wondered why I couldn't have been brave enough to ask her out in high school. If I had married her instead of Amanda, things would probably have worked out much better. She at least seemed to care about my needs and feelings.

It was such a tender moment that I leaned over and gave her a kiss. It wasn't a romantic kiss. It was a kiss that said, "Thank you and goodbye." She knew it and I did, too. I was encouraged by her strength, her concern, and her belief in me. Maybe I could do this. Maybe I was strong enough to get through this mess and come out better on the other side.

However, before I could even finish processing the thought, life stabbed me right in the middle of my back. It was a vicious blow that took my breath away. Something in my peripheral vision caught my eye, and I turned to see Amanda sitting in her car watching us.

I called to her and tried to tell her it wasn't what she thought, but she had already made up her mind. She rolled her car window down and told me I had thirty minutes to get home, gather my stuff, and get out. If I wasn't out by then, she would start throwing my belongings out the door.

Not wanting Jacki to get involved in our dilemma, I told her to go check on her kids. She gave me a concerned look before rushing away. I wanted to run after her, but I knew the right thing to do was to try to pacify my irate wife. I walked over to her car, and she repeated herself.

"Thirty minutes, Jacob," she said, as she put the pedal to the floor and took off.

My mind was a blur, and I wasn't sure what to do next. I had planned on packing anyway, so maybe that was the thing to do. Just go home, pack my belongings, and head to my mother's house.

However, I wasn't quite ready to head home and face the wrath of Amanda, so I stopped at the local convenience store to buy a pack of cigarettes. I was shaking so badly that the cashier noticed and asked if I was alright. I told her, "Not really," but thanked her for her concern.

I went out and sat in the car for awhile to try to clear my brain. Everything was a blur, and I couldn't seem to organize my thoughts. I didn't want to go home. I didn't really care if Amanda and I broke up anymore. She didn't seem to want to try, and home wasn't home without Rex. Maybe there wasn't anything left to save.

Thoughts of my mom and our conversation that morning came to mind. I was so happy to have reconnected with her after so many years apart, and going to stay with her for awhile seemed like a viable option. I wanted her to be proud of me, just like Grammy and Grampy Miller had always been.

Thinking of my Miller grandparents filled me with a sense of emptiness. I truly missed them. I knew they were in Heaven and at peace. The thought of them relaxing on a cloud brought a smile to my face, and also changed my thought process. They had found the peace that I wanted. I was tired of struggling, and I would enjoy floating on a cloud with them.

I reached over and opened the glove box on the passenger side. Yes, the gun was still there. I had almost forgotten about it, but right now, it could be a useful tool for me. Maybe going to the ball park where I had played so many games, longing for my mother to be on the bleachers cheering for me, might give me the courage to end it all. Just looking at those empty bleachers and thinking about all the losses in my life might be just what I needed to give me the courage to pull the trigger.

Having made my decision, I laid the gun in my lap and started the car. The ball field wasn't far away, and I almost smiled in relief, knowing my problems were about to end. Little did I know, but life had one more nasty surprise in store for me.

I drove through the narrow streets of Newton Falls, the place that I had called home for the last few years, but nothing was really visible. My brain was still going faster than what I could keep up with, and the activity of life around me was just a blur. All I knew was that I had to make it to the ball field at the end of town, and then my problems would all be over.

There were a couple of intersections between the convenience store and the ball field, and with my mind so pre-occupied, I failed to negotiate the rules of the road. Apparently the light had turned red, but I never even saw it. The loud blast of a car horn broke through my thoughts, and I stared in surprise at the car located within inches of my door. We had almost crashed!

The jolt brought a bit of sense back to me. While I wanted to end my own life, I certainly didn't want to cause harm to anyone else. Yet, in my current state of mind, that is exactly what could have happened. I realized I wasn't safe to be driving. It reminded me of the time we had left the Rapini party in defeat and Amanda had to drive for me. But she wasn't here this time. I was on my own.

I decided I needed to at least pull over to the side of the road and let the cars pass by. Maybe when the traffic cleared, I could slowly make my way to the ball field. However, when I pulled over, not all of the traffic passed. The car I had almost struck pulled up quickly behind me. I jumped out to apologize and tell them I hadn't meant to run the red light, but these people didn't seem interested in a friendly chat.

What happened next has never really been clear to me. It was almost like viewing the scene through a kaleidoscope, with multiple versions of the same couple of people confronting me and not being able to tell which ones were real. Maybe it was the marijuana that was still fresh in my system, along with the fact that I hadn't slept all night long, that caused things to seem so distorted.

I could tell there were two angry people approaching me, one from each side of the car. The driver was heavy set and angry, charging at me like they wanted to kill me. The passenger was not quite as aggressive, but seemed ready to back up the actions of the driver.

It appeared to be two men, both of them moving aggressively my way, with lots of unfriendly, derogative names flowing freely from their mouths. I had no arguments with them. I just wanted to jump in my car in fear and drive away, which is exactly what I should have done. No matter what I said, they didn't seem to be stopping. I was scared to the core. I was ready to die, but I wanted it to be at my own hand, not at the hands of some strangers I didn't even know.

In my troubled brain, all I could think was that they were coming after me, and their intentions were not good. I yelled at them, "Stop, stop, stop!!" I even heard the sound to go with my words. However, it didn't take long to realize it wasn't my imagination. The sound was too clear and realistic. It almost echoed through my head.

It was my gun going off! "Pop, pop, pop!!" Apparently, I had grabbed it while exiting the car and had it in my hand.

I didn't even realize I had shot anyone until the driver started to fall. With my distorted vision, I'm surprised I hit anyone at all. Those years of target practice in my father's back yard had unfortunately paid off. As the subject fell, I saw the pony tail sticking out of the back of her baseball cap and realized that I had just shot a woman! The passenger, apparently her boyfriend, had retreated back to the car and ducked down behind the dash.

When I realized what I had done, the desire to end my life was stronger than ever. Apparently in my current frame of mind, I had emptied the whole clip of my gun. I dove into my car and frantically dug through my glove box to find another clip. I reloaded the gun, put it to my head, and pulled the trigger. However, the gun misfired and didn't do the intended job.

"What!" my brain screamed in frustration. "I can't even kill myself and do it right!"

I looked around and realized people had started gathering to see what the commotion was all about. Suddenly, someone was there, trying to take the gun out of my hand. Somehow Amanda had found out what was happening. Had she been following me? Was she really here? Or was this all just a bad dream, a nightmare of nightmares that I would wake up from in a cold sweat and be glad that it wasn't real? What was real, and what wasn't? Everything was a blur, and I couldn't tell anymore.

One thing quickly became clear, though. This was no dream. If I had wanted to end my life, it seemed that whatever had just happened had successfully completed the task. A stranger named Sierra McGovern lay dead on the ground, and I was the one holding the smoking gun.

CHAPTER 10
A Judicial Joke

We have all heard the saying, "Innocent until proven guilty." It was something I had always believed in, although I had never had anything to do with the judicial system.

All my life, I had managed to remain a law-abiding citizen. My contact with law enforcement had only amounted to a traffic ticket or two. I had never been involved in a crime, let alone a serious or life altering one. It seemed to me that my lack of criminal history would attest to my successful upbringing and beliefs.

Yet, after that fateful night, I realized that a person isn't always innocent until proven guilty. In my case, I was guilty from the moment I pulled the trigger. Yes, I had shot Sierra McGovern. I wouldn't deny that, nor could I deny it. The proof was there. But the why, or how, or any of the reasons for what had caused it to occur were of no consequence. I had done the evil deed, and the legal system was going to make sure I paid for it.

I had tasted my last bite of freedom. There was no bail set for me. I was thrown into prison with every intention of keeping me there. My reputation for following the law during the past thirty-two years of my life seemed to be of little importance. The judge wasn't going to give me any opportunities to return to whatever home I might have had at that point. He considered me to be a threat to society, and so I would remain in jail until my trial.

It was a discouraging thought, but I hoped when the time for my trial arrived, the jury would see that I was a good person. I had just been caught in an incredibly bad series of events which had left me mentally distraught. It had been a perfect storm, really, and the outcome had been a devastating one.

Hopefully, they would become aware of that and realize I was not a terrible person with violent tendencies. I had heard about people experiencing temporary insanity and had always thought it wasn't possible. But, now it had happened to me. Now I knew that it was real, and that it could happen to anyone.

The goal of the State's Attorney was to prove that I had intended to kill Sierra McGovern. I was somewhat relieved when I heard that. I had never meant any harm to her. I didn't even know her, and I certainly had nothing against her. Why would I want to kill a stranger I didn't even know? That was simply not a part of my nature. Surely my trial would prove that to the jury, and make it clear that killing Sierra had just been a terrible, horrific accident.

However, there was little about my trial that was fair. Right from the start, it was clear to see that things were not going to go well for me. The first problem occurred when those in charge of the trial location decided to hold it in the same small town where the crime had taken place.

How was it possible to get even the slightest chance of a fair trial in a situation like that? This was a rural town with a population of less than 7,000. There was no one in this town that hadn't heard about the crime and already formed an opinion. This was their little town, and they were going to do all they could to protect it from criminals like me. To receive a fair trial, it should have taken place in a city away from the scene of the crime, where the senses of protection and preservation were not so strong, and it would have been easier to find unbiased jurors.

As far as the "speedy" part goes, well, my trial was definitely "speedy." They had said it would take about three weeks and have dozens of witnesses.   What happened in reality was that it took longer to pick the jury members than the trial itself lasted. My mom and dad were right there for me through the whole process, though. That was the best part of the trial – getting to see my family. I had missed having daily contact with them during my days of incarceration. Knowing they were sitting behind me as a show of support was very reassuring to me.

The judge and lawyers made me feel as though I was an active part of choosing the jury, but I actually had little to say about it. They made the decisions. What could I do to change anything? After the jury had been chosen, I found myself frequently glancing their way and wondering what had happened. Gazing across the jury of twelve, I realized that most of them had white hair or were bald. They could easily have been called a jury of my parents' peers, but definitely not mine. Only one of them was even close to my age and, ironically, they made her the spokesperson.

I wondered how this jury of my parents' peers could relate to what had happened in my life. Drug use and the need to carry a gun had not been prominent issues in their lifetime. Their generation had lived a more

reserved and sheltered lifestyle, where these situations weren't as pronounced. I only hoped that my lawyer would do a good job representing
me, and help them to understand what had gone wrong in my life that
brought me from the status of a law-abiding citizen to that of a murderer.

However, my lawyer did little to fight for me. In fact, it almost
seemed at times as though he was afraid of the female judge. When she
would question him, he would stutter and grow embarrassed. He often
mumbled, was sometimes hard to hear, and frequently backed down from
a challenge. Plus, he didn't address questionable statements made by the
prosecution or any of the witnesses, even when they were controversial
remarks. If he hadn't had white hair and a history of experience, I would
have thought that this was one of his first trials.

The "dozens of witnesses" turned out to be more like six. My wife
testified, even though she was no longer my wife by that point. The trial
took place close to two years after the crime, which threw out the original
thought of being entitled to a speedy trial. Amanda had begun those two
years as a devoted wife, coming every week during visitation to spend time
with me. But somewhere along the way, things had fallen apart and she
had stopped coming so often.

At first I thought I couldn't survive without her visits, but then it
all came to a head. We had a bad fight, and that was it. Her visitations
stopped altogether and I found I didn't miss her as much as I thought I
would. After that, she had filed for divorce and taken her maiden name
back.

At the trial, she was very supportive, though. She testified about
how painful my illness had been, how I had sometimes been known to curl
up in a ball on the floor due to the excruciating pain. She didn't point out
all my faults or flaws. She didn't bring our personal disagreements into any
part of her testimony, or claim that I was not a good husband or person
because of my weaknesses. She only supported the fact that I had a sometimes debilitating illness and that life had been difficult for me to manage
because of it.

Jacki was also called to be a witness. I watched her on the witness
stand with mixed emotions. It was so good to see her again, and I wanted
to run up and give her a hug. But on the other hand, it broke my heart that
she had to be there. She should never have had to be a part of this mess I
had made. I felt bad that she had been placed in such a stressful situation,
but I was proud of how well she handled herself. She was fair and true, and
just as supportive as my wife had been.

The prosecution called Sierra's boyfriend to testify. He denied getting out of the car, and yet my lawyer never challenged him. If he had stayed in the car, the whole thing might not have even happened. I had seen two men charging at me that day, and the need to defend myself had kicked in and caused me to overreact. I felt that this was an important issue, and one that my lawyer should have brought to light, but he never even pointed out that her boyfriend had lied under oath. I wanted to jump up and shout, "You're lying!" But, my lawyer just let it all slide by, as though it was insignificant information.

Two psychiatrists testified as well, one of them in support of my situation, and one of them as a member of the prosecuting team. Dr. Jones did a great job for me. He truly understood what had happened. He knew that my brain was not working properly on that terrible day. He knew that when a brain encounters a crisis, it can freeze, or shut down. This causes it to be unable to process surrounding information adequately enough to allow for an appropriate response.

That is exactly what had happened to me. My brain had been on overload. I had too much happening in my life at the time of the crisis. I had just lost Jacki for good. My wife was kicking me out. I had lost everything – my home, my job, my income, my dog, and ultimately, my life. Suicide had seemed the best solution for me, yet before I had a chance to do it, I found myself in a crisis like I had never faced before, staring at two angry strangers who seemed intent on killing me.

I was truly appreciative of Dr. Jones' support and his willingness to share his professional opinion. He made an honest attempt at trying to help everyone, jurors and judge included, to understand what I was going through. But before I could even bask in a state of gratitude for his assistance on my behalf, they called Dr. Chipmunk to the stand. And what he had to say shot down any victory I may have felt from the support offered by Dr. Jones.

Of course, his name wasn't really Dr. Chipmunk. It was a nickname my family gave him, not because of his personality so much, but because of something he had done. When taking the seat to testify, he went on for about ten minutes, bragging about all of his accomplishments and the education he had received in his lifetime. I waited for someone to tell him that was enough and he could stop at any time, but no one did. They just let him rant and rave about himself.

However, a little later during his testimony, he had to pause and wait while the lawyers consulted with the judge. While he waited, he cupped his hands together in front of him, looking a lot like a little chipmunk holding a nut in its paws. It really looked quite foolish, and I wished I could have taken a picture of it. So, to my family, he became known as Dr. Chipmunk. The name seemed to fit, because he was a mousy little man, and it helped us to vent our frustration and anger a small fraction for the damage he caused.

Ultimately, what Dr. Chipmunk did was to use his position of power to sway the jurors, who had probably already made up their minds before entering the courtroom anyway. They had come longing to find me guilty. They weren't concerned about what had happened in my life or the reason the crime had occurred. They were only seeking vengeance. So, he gave them what they wanted. When asked by the prosecuting attorney if I had intended to kill Sierra McGovern, Dr. Chipmunk had stated, in a matter-of-fact kind of way, "Of course he did. He pulled the trigger, didn't he?"

I had never been a violent person. I was not one to sit around and think violent thoughts. I didn't plot or plan ways to hurt other people, even while I had sat idly in a jail cell for the past two years, thinking of all that had happened and waiting to share my side of the story. For all the times when my wife had beaten and abused me, I simply tolerated it and never fought back. I had never formed any thoughts of retaliation against her, only accepted my beatings like a humble, wounded puppy, waiting for the abuse to end.

However, when Dr. Chipmunk said I intended to kill Sierra simply because I had pulled the trigger, it was all I could do to sit still and tolerate it. I wanted to jump out of my seat, leap over the table, sprint across the courtroom, and make that little rodent of a man prove that he truly was a psychiatrist. I wanted to shake my finger in his mousy little face and tell him to take that statement back, because a true psychiatrist would know that it wasn't that cut and dry. I didn't possess a doctor's degree, but I knew the brain was more complicated than that. How could he, with all his qualifications as a psychiatric doctor, make it all sound so simple?

During my past two years in jail, I had done some studies on the brain. What Dr. Jones had said was true. The brain is a complex organism, and with all that was going through mine that fateful day, there was no way I could have adequately processed what was happening and make rational or appropriate decisions. It had all happened so quickly, within about thirty seconds of time. My brain was a jumbled up mess. Yet, here was a doctor, claiming to be a psychiatric expert, stating it was as simple as deciding whether or not to pull the trigger.

The State's Attorney seemed to gloat over Dr. Chipmunk's answer. He quickly finished his inquiries and took a seat. I waited for my lawyer to challenge what had just been said and to put Dr. Chipmunk in his place. I wanted him to make the jury see that things were more convoluted than that. However, my head spun in confusion when he declined to ask any further questions and let Dr. Chipmunk's opinion stand unchallenged.

Wasn't he my lawyer? Wasn't he supposed to believe in me and fight for me? His role was to try to establish reasonable doubt on my behalf. Shouldn't he at least have pointed out my emotional condition at the time and dug a little deeper into Dr. Chipmunk's statement? But he had just let the prosecution gain a major victory, and possibly a triumphant ending to the whole trial.

Dr. Chipmunk had failed to take into consideration that my body and brain were not on speaking terms that horrific day. My lawyer should have pointed that out and challenged the validity of his statement. He should have reviewed what Dr. Jones had said and questioned how Dr. Chipmunk's opinion could vary so much.

Dr. Jones was a legitimate psychiatrist, too. My lawyer should have at least made Dr. Chipmunk's testimony sound questionable to the jury, but he failed to do so. He simply let it rest, leaving the scales tipped extremely unfavorably, and possibly irretrievably, against me.

There were only a few more witnesses called during the trial. Of course, the fitness guru was called, both because he was an eyewitness at the scene and because he was a police officer. One other eyewitness was called, who had little to offer, but that was it. No character witnesses that could attest to who I was prior to the crime, or the fact that I was a law-abiding, family-oriented man who had successfully participated in life for thirty-two years. It was like they just wanted to get this trial over and done with so they could move on to something else.

The fine citizens of Newton Falls just wanted to put this all behind them and be done with it. The sooner they could get this processed, the more likely they would be able to return to normalcy in their little town. It was their job to make sure a troublemaker like me wouldn't get away with upsetting the tranquility of their peaceful, little town, and they were going to make sure they didn't fail.

The day they found me guilty, my mother cried like I have never heard her cry before. Her wails of agony echoed down the hallways of the courthouse. She had known that I did not intend to kill Sierra McGovern, and she had counted on the legal system to help us wade through these murky waters to prove it. We both felt as though we had been let down. We knew that in a different courtroom, in a different setting, with a different legal team, and with someone who would have fought for us, the jury would have seen that it was all a horrific, appalling mistake.

Not that I wanted to get away with the crime. I knew that I deserved punishment, but I had already been sitting in a jail cell in different locations throughout the state for the last two years. During that time, I had hoped and prayed for the opportunity to show society that I was not a vicious animal who was out seeking to destroy innocent people. I wanted them to understand me, what caused this horrible crime, and to see that it could happen to anyone. But when all was said and done, none of it mattered. I was guilty and society was going to make me pay for what I had done.

When it came time for my sentencing hearing, my mother was unable to attend. At first, I was extremely disappointed. She had been to every hearing and attended every day of my trial. Even though it was a six-hour drive for her to get there, she had made the necessary arrangements to be there to support me through all of it. But something unforeseen had come up, and there was no way she could make it to the sentencing.

However, that proved to be a blessing in disguise. During my Pre-Sentence Investigation, my family had been good at supporting me. They had all written letters, supporting my lack of violent tendencies and my history of having been a law-abiding citizen.

When the judge began her argument during my Sentencing Hearing, she referred to those letters and said that I had a very supportive family. Her speech began so well, that I was quite encouraged. She went on to say that I had a low-to-moderate chance of being a re-offender. And then she slapped me with a forty-two year sentence!

If my mom had wailed when they found me guilty, I have no idea what she would have done upon hearing the forty-two year sentence. She probably wouldn't have been able to contain herself. She either would have burst into tears in the courtroom, or might have even stood up and challenged the judge herself. All I can say is that I am thankful she was spared hearing the news firsthand.

That was one of the worst days of my life. Not only did my life get taken completely away from me that day, with little chance of being able to retrieve it, but I had to sit and endure the wrath of Sierra McGovern's family. On that day, they read letters they had written to me, expressing their anger. They condemned me for talking and acting happy with my family in the courtroom. They claimed I was laughing and joking with my family, like none of this mattered and I wasn't taking it seriously.

Seriously?! My contact with my family had been very limited during the past two years while I had been incarcerated. I had been excited to make eye contact with them and be allowed to communicate briefly during breaks in the courtroom. I didn't think I had spent a lot of time laughing and joking with them. And I certainly didn't see any of this as humorous - not in any way, shape, or manner. This was my life, my future, my destination. How could I not take it seriously?

Some of the confrontations were so intense that my lawyer's assistant had to link arms with me and try to hold me in my seat. I just wanted to get up and run. Did they think I intended to kill Sierra? Did they think I had wanted to take their daughter away from them, to leave a little girl to grow up without her mother, and to cause such heartache and disruption in their family?

I knew what it felt like to lose a family member suddenly and un-expectedly. I knew the pain, the heartache, and the intense empty feeling associated with such a loss. Losing Little Shay had left a hole in my heart that would never mend. I would never intentionally inflict that kind of pain on others, especially a family that I didn't even know. Perhaps they all believed what Dr. Chipmunk had said, and that I had intended to kill Sierra simply because I had pulled the trigger.

I wanted to stand up and defend myself, to shout to the world and everyone in the courtroom that I was sorry and that I would do anything to change the outcome. This is not what I had wanted to happen in my life or to Sierra McGovern's family. Having heard the forty-two year sentence, I would have given anything to be able to grab my gun and make it success-fully to the ball field, where I could have ended it all and rid myself of this nightmare.

After listening to the McGovern family beat up on me for what seemed like just short of forever, I was given a few moments to speak. I stood and read my message to them, asking them to forgive me, and telling them how sorry I was. I know my words sounded weak and insignificant in light of all they had been through, but it was all I had to offer. I tried to bravely read my statement, but I had trouble seeing what I had written through my tears, and my voice broke with emotion.

And then they put the shackles back on my hands and feet and led me from the courtroom, back to the jail cell that had become my home. I had never felt so forsaken in all my life. Prior to this, I had held to the belief that maybe I would be given something to hope for.

Typically, a second-degree manslaughter charge comes with a twenty year sentence. While that was a long time to think about, at least it was doable. With a forty-two year sentence, there was no hope. Between my physical condition and the fact that I was now 34 years old, there was no way I would ever taste freedom again.

Liberty and justice for all? Well, maybe justice for some, but unfortunately, not for me. If only my gun had not misfired on that fateful day. Or if I could have made it to the ball field, my problems could have ended two years ago. Now I had nothing left but a lifetime of shackles, incarceration, and misery to look forward to.

CHAPTER 11
Prison Daze

Free room and board, that's how I had sometimes heard people describe prison life. I think that anyone who could believe that must not have had much of a lifestyle to begin with. The quality of their way of life prior to jail time must have been extremely poor to be able to remain satisfied with the state of incarceration. Or perhaps, for those who had never experienced prison life firsthand, they only fantasized that imprisonment was a free way of living and not that bad.

It didn't take long to discovered how awful prison life was. I was not accustomed to being confined to a small, windowless, cement block, and I had to share it with another person as well. It was stifling, both physically and emotionally. Before this, I had always been independent, capable, and usually successful at making my own daily decisions. Yet, one thirty-second encounter in which I had made a devastating mistake had taken it all away. I was no longer independent, and my skills of being capable and successful were now used simply to keep myself safe, alive, and trying not to upset fellow inmates.

Prior to my trial, I was incarcerated in local State facilities, where most of the other prisoners had committed minimal crimes. However, once I was convicted of Second-Degree Murder, I found myself moved out-of-state and housed in larger facilities with other murderers and rapists. These proved to be wicked individuals. They were people who had no values in life, who had fire in their eyes, and pure evil in their souls. They had had to fight all of their lives merely to survive, so an aggressive way of life was all they knew.

I got weary of the constant fights in prison. I had never been an aggressive person, yet if I didn't fight to defend myself, these evil beings would walk all over me. I found out that in prison, morals are nonexistent and values are reversed. For prison life, good is bad and bad becomes good. The greater the crime you had committed, the bigger a hero you were hailed as. Prisoners admired those who had done horrific crimes and could boast of unspeakable acts of malice. Some of the crimes these men had committed were beyond the scope of my wildest, mind-boggling imaginations. Yet, they laughed and joked about them, as though committing such hideous acts on humanity were an every day occurrence and nothing to be concerned about.

I often wondered how I could ever have found myself housed with individuals such as these. It was frequently hard to even think of them as human beings. To be a human meant that one had to possess an essence of human nature, but these men had committed some inconceivable, appalling deeds, and, yet, were light-hearted about what they had done. No, these were not at all men. A lot of them ranked not much higher on the food chain than that of a vicious, wild animal.

Oh, they weren't all bad. Occasionally, I would find myself sharing a cell with another person who had only been caught in a bad situation, like I had. Some of my cell mates actually had morals and values, too. Those were the days that weren't so bad. However, since their crimes were not as intense as some, they didn't stay around long. They would usually get released quickly, or transferred to another facility where the security wasn't as strict. But I seemed forever caught in the same situation, with little chance of ever being moved to a less restrictive environment.

When I was in my home state prisons, where my family could occasionally visit, I was in somewhat more familiar territory. I bounced around from prison to prison there, but at least the prisons were all within traveling distance for my family. However, once I became a convicted felon, I was a ward of the state, and their goal was to house me as cheaply as possible. So they outsourced their prisoners to other states, believing it was the cheapest way to care for them. And "cheap," as we all know, does not usually pertain to "quality."

The first place they shipped me to was a prison several states away from home, which I came to refer to as "The Viking Ship." This was a prison that seemed to be lost in time, which is where The Viking Ship idea came from. It was like a ship from long ago that had sailed off to battle, had gotten lost along the way, and never found its way back home. And the funny thing is that no one seemed to miss it or know that it even still existed. This prison was located out in the middle of nowhere. I sometimes thought the only people who knew this prison existed were the guards who showed up at work each day!

The biggest change I noticed right away was the loneliness from missing my family. Their visits had come to a halt, as the prison was not within easy traveling distance for them. In order for them to visit, they

would have to take time off from work and fly out specifically for the purpose of visiting me. And, since there was nothing special about this area,
it wasn't like it was even an attractive vacation destination.

Compared to the prisons back home, this one proved much more
challenging. Perhaps it was learning to mingle with prisoners from other
states, those who had different cultures, beliefs, and lifestyles, that was
so difficult. It was like the melting pot of America, with prisoners from all
walks of life. Back at the prisons in my own home state, they had all just
been country bumpkins like me. Most of them hadn't done anything terribly serious, and we had a form of understanding that was hard to establish
with these new inmates.

I found throughout the years that the transition from one prison to
another never went smoothly. It was a lesson I learned quickly. With this
first move, I experienced a lot of frustration. Just prior to leaving my home
state, my dad had bought me a nice pair of sneakers. He knew he wouldn't
see me for awhile, since he was not a traveler and never left home, so he
wanted to get me something that would last for awhile.

It was a nice parting gift that I knew I would cherish for years to
come. However, upon arriving at my new location, it soon became clear
that not all my belongings had followed me. I never did see those sneakers again, and my tablet that allowed me to communicate with my mother
didn't materialize either. It made me wonder if guards somewhere along
the way rummaged through our belongings, picking and choosing what
they could keep for themselves as souvenirs. And one of them had claimed
a nice pair of brand new sneakers as their own. My tablet did finally reap-
pear, but it took months of aggravation and multiple calls from my mother
to track it down. In the meantime, my only form of communication was
the few phone calls I was allowed to make, which were few and far between. With my tablet, use was limited, but I could at least communicate
through emails.

Although this prison seemed antiquated and remote, I realized later in time that those were not necessarily bad traits for a prison to have.
My mother and one of my aunt's did eventually fly out to visit me for a
couple of days. They joked that if anyone escaped from this prison, they
would return. It was located in such a remote area that there was nothing
to survive on out there. They said there was nothing but trees and wilder-
ness beyond the chain link fencing and barbed wire that surrounded my
new home.

The food at The Viking Ship was not very good either. It consisted
of various forms of beans – baked beans, string beans, three bean salad, or

lima beans. They tried many different ways to disguise them, but it all just tasted like beans. However, I began to realize that by controlling my diet, I could control the pancreatic symptoms. Not that I really had much control over my diet, though. I either ate what they served me, or I went to bed hungry. If my mom had extra money, I could ask her to order some food for me from the Commissary, but I couldn't always count on that.

One bad experience at this prison will stay with me for the rest of my life. It happened just days before my mother was supposed to arrive for her visit. I had only a few earthly possessions, and nothing that I would really have considered to be valuable. Yet, one thing I had that another prisoner wanted was my MP3 player. It was old and outdated, but it was at least a distraction that gave me some relief from the stressors of prison life.

Just prior to our scheduled visit, one of my cell mates held a knife to my throat and demanded I give him the player. It was my introduction to the hardcore life of prison and being housed with men who have no values. At first, I was surprised that he possessed a knife in prison. However, it didn't take long for me to realize that you can get anything you want in prison. You just need to know who to make the proper connection with.

I said nothing to the guards about this interaction. I simply let him have the MP3 player and determined I would get another one. If I ratted him out, I might be the one to get punished. Somehow, the incident might get blamed on me, and if I ended up in solitary confinement, I would miss out on my visit. I couldn't let that happen. The player could be replaced, but who knew how long before my family would be allowed another opportunity to visit.

Prison life taught me a lot of things that I wouldn't have learned otherwise, and not necessarily good traits. One thing this experience taught me was to never have anything worth stealing. If I owned nothing of value, my life wouldn't be placed in jeopardy for trying to protect it.

Another thing it taught me was the art of negotiating. Maybe we didn't possess much in prison, but we learned to wheel and deal what we did have. I was constantly trading things with other inmates, partly to satisfy them so they would leave me alone, and partly to get the things I needed. As much as I hated the thought, I frequently found myself paying them off to buy me some safety and peace of mind. If I failed to make a promised payment, I would sometimes find myself in a state of physical, debilitating pain.

And that is another thing prison life taught me – how to inflict pain on others. I learned ways to quickly bring people to their knees in agony which, as mentioned before, wasn't necessarily a good trait to learn. But in prison, it was a lifesaver. Without knowing these moves and defenses, I would have been completely vulnerable. With all the years of abuse from my wife, I had always avoided retaliation and inflicting pain on others. But in prison, it became necessary as a means of survival.

I was transferred to a couple of other prisons after The Viking Ship experience. When their contract ran out after a few years time, I was sent to a prison closer to my mother's location. That proved to be a bittersweet experience. The good part was that my mother was able to visit frequently, since it was only about four hours from her home. I cherished those visits with my mother. One time, she even brought Little Ricky with her. That was an amazing visit.

This prison had better food than the Viking Ship and allowed access to the library. Both of those were real bonuses for me. The food didn't cause as many physical complications, which made trips to the bathroom occur less frequently, and the use of the library was awesome. I loved studying, and found I spent many hours at the library. However, the guards at this location were all on an ego trip. They acted like they thought they were superhuman, and we were the scum of the earth. Because of their attitudes, there were a lot of fights between the guards and the prisoners.

Several of the inmates from my home state died at this prison, for one reason or another, so the governor actually broke the contract and sent us packing again. While I was relieved to get out of that atmosphere, I was disappointed to find that they were sending us further south, to a new facility located more than twenty hours away from home. I knew the chances of ever seeing my family during my stay there would be pretty slim.

Fear and despair soon became my two prominent emotions. I feared for my safety almost every minute of every day in this new facility. I learned that things worked much better if I slept all day long and stayed awake at night instead. There was less chaos and confusion to deal with that way. But I always slept with my back up against the wall, both as a means of self-preservation and also to be facing whatever danger might be coming my way.

The sense of despair was almost overwhelming most of the time. What point was there in even getting out of bed each day, other than to eat and go to the bathroom? I knew all I would do was stare at the same ugly walls again tomorrow.

With more than a forty year sentence, I would be incarcerated for the rest of my life. There was no counting down the days until my release.

I would probably die before my sentence was completed, either from my medical problems or from the prison violence.

Oh, we had tried jumping through all the hoops and filing whatever paperwork we could to try to get my sentence reduced. It seemed somebody somewhere should have realized that my sentence had been extreme. I should have been charged with Unintentional Second-Degree Murder, or possibly Second-Degree Manslaughter. These would have carried a sentence of fifteen-to-twenty years. But even the letters to the governor, lawyers, appeals, and filing a PCR (Post Conviction Relief) proved to be of little avail. It was like society had filed me away, expecting me to spend the rest of my life rotting away in a God-forsaken jail cell.

I found it increasingly difficult to crawl out of bed day after day. It reminded me of the days when Rex was the only reason I had to drag myself out from beneath my blankets each morning. But at least back then, I still had my freedom. I could go to the park, or the store, or wherever Amanda had allowed me to. Now I had nowhere to go and nothing to do.

The thought of Rex always brought tears to my eyes. I missed that dog. He had been my best friend, or even better than a friend, if that was possible. He had been like my soulmate and had stood by me through thick or thin. He was faithful and true, no matter what my shortcomings had been. I often wondered how life had turned out for him. I'm sure Sarah loved him and took good care of him, but I would never get over how Amanda had given him away like she did. If she hadn't done so, I probably wouldn't have been sitting behind bars now, housed in a cement block building, and surrounded by barbed wire.

The thought of never seeing Rex again always stirred up other emotions within me. I would think of my mother's parents, how they were getting older and how I would probably never see them again. I thought of Kelli, my dad, of Ricky and Nicole, and my Rapini siblings. Would I ever see any of them again, the family that had been such a part of my life and given me the cherished memories that got me through these days of despair? How long would I remain in this "hell on earth" situation? Would there ever be a chance of my sentence being reduced and having an opportunity to taste freedom again?

If only they would transfer me back closer to home. If I could at least see a relative or two occasionally, it might give me hope enough to hang on. But yet, I was powerless to do anything to change the situation. I was at the mercy of the judicial system, which seemed to have forgotten that I even existed.

Free room and board? I determined if I ever heard anyone say anything like that, I would immediately speak up and let them know exactly what I thought about it. I could tell them firsthand just what this free room and board was like. No, I would never take freedom for granted again. Freedom - was it something I would ever be allowed the opportunity to experience again?

CHAPTER 12
Reflections

They say hindsight is 20/20, and I came to understand firsthand what that meant. With an abundance of free time on my hands, I had plenty of opportunity to reflect on my life, determine what had gone wrong, and think about the things I could have done differently.

Day after day of sitting behind metal bars in an empty, lonely, cement cell allowed my mind the time and freedom to reflect. Sometimes I thought so much, my brain hurt and I felt like my head would explode. There were times when I just wanted to run, to sprint down these forsaken hallways that echoed with hollow despair. I wanted to flee these bleak, barren rows of inmate cells and just run away from it all. If only I could find relief from my thoughts, my failures, my shortcomings, and the sins of the past that had brought me to this desolate place that I now called home.

I spent a lot of time thinking back on my childhood. As I did, I realized there wasn't much I could have changed there. Of course, it wasn't all bad. I had plenty of happy childhood memories, and that is probably what got me through the bad times. But ultimately, I came to terms with the fact that I was a child, and that had left me at the mercy of those who had charge over me. How could I have possibly changed anything in my childhood?

There is no way I could have kept my parents from divorcing. That was the first crisis I faced, and at a very tender age, too. I had relied heavily on Kelli to help me through those days until mom had settled down and married Paul. Then life had been so good that I hadn't wanted anything to ever change. But change it did when Little Shay left us. Though the memory of her passing all those years ago still brought tears to my eyes, I knew there is absolutely nothing that I could have done to protect and save her. How could anyone ever have foreseen a tragedy of that magnitude, or kept it from happening? It was a freak accident, an anomaly, something that just plain shouldn't have happened, but did anyway.

While I didn't think I would ever recover from the pain of losing

Little Shay, things only got worse when my mother moved away. It felt like that was the final blow that would make my world fall apart. The life I had loved was gone, and life at dad's was so quiet and empty compared to what I had become accustomed to.

Yet, again, I was still a child. Maybe I was an older child, but I still needed the love and support of both parents. Being older this time, it was harder to rely on Kelli to fill the void. She had so much going on in her own life that I couldn't expect her to be there for all my problems. Plus, she wasn't a mother. I couldn't expect to confide in her and seek advice the way a teenage boy would look to his mother for guidance.

Again, I came to terms with the fact that there was nothing I could have done to change any of it. I had the love and memories of the happy Rapini family days to get me through the rest of my childhood and move on to graduate from both high school and college. It was those happy memories that gave me the resiliency to push forward and not give up.

Then I had been confronted with my chance at adulthood and life on my own. Did I have the stamina and ability to be successful in life? Was I capable of surviving on my own and able to support a wife and a household? Had I planned and prepared enough to be self-sufficient?

I had absolutely loved my career choice. I had never shied away from a challenge, and computers had definitely tested my ability. Maybe it was my childhood traumas that had taught me to be resilient and persevere, even in the face of adversity. And working with computers, I often found myself facing adversity! But I tackled each problem with fervor, and a determination to not be defeated by a piece of technology. Man had created the computer, so man should be able to solve whatever problem he encountered with it.

Yes, I had thrived on my career and the challenges that had come along with it. Although there were times when those small boxes full of electrodes had just about driven me crazy, I had still loved my job. Losing it had been a devastating blow. Not just a financial blow, but an assault to my ego. I was a capable person, and a very dependable employee, until my body had fallen apart and changed all of that.

Once again, it wasn't something I had much control over. I had rarely called in sick, even on the days when it was all I could do to crawl out of bed. I wanted to work. I didn't want to sit around the house in agony and be ruled by the demands of my body. Working had helped to keep my mind occupied and off any problems I might have been facing at the time.

My failing health was the beginning of my downfall. I had never known such physical pain before. There were times when all I could do was curl up in a ball on the floor and groan in agony. Since I didn't understand at the time what was wrong or how to help myself, I naturally felt that medication was the cure. But the more I took, the more I wanted. I feared having the pain come back again, and overusing my medication seemed to be the solution. How wrong I was.

After I entered the prison system, I learned that my symptoms could be managed, to a certain degree, with a proper diet. Yet, I was still at the mercy of the prison cafeteria. I didn't enjoy going to bed hungry, but I had to choose. Which was worse? Not eating and dealing with hunger pains, or indulging in something that would ultimately cause me to be in agony the next day with extended stays in the bathroom? I usually chose the hunger pains.

Of course, there were things I could have done prior to my jail time to either help myself, or have avoided altogether, so as not to cause the problem in the first place. If I had stayed away from the alcohol, I might not have encountered so much pancreatic pain. I had come to realize it was a recurrent alcoholic pancreatitis, but even when I had become aware of the connection between the two, it was hard to stop myself. The alcohol was my release in life, my way of avoiding the emotional pain I was facing. But instead, it caused physical pain and issues that sent me into a tailspin which I couldn't seem to recover from. It was a real dilemma for me.

When I did lose my job, I could have put more effort into establishing a home-based business. I knew computers well, so I could have set up a shop at home doing computer repair. Or maybe I could have pursued some of my other interests, like small engine repair, or some form of business pertaining to guns and hunting supplies. If I had only found a way to help support my family financially, Amanda wouldn't have been so hard on me. The abuse might not have occurred and caused all the anger to build up inside until I was ready to explode.

And then, there's the affair with Jacki. What can I say about that? If I hadn't been married to Amanda and been in so much emotional turmoil over the affair, I would have said it was one of the happiest times of my life. Jacki had made me feel loved and like a man again. I have often kicked myself for not being brave enough to ask her out back in high school. If I had, life could have turned out completely different. She was loving and kind to me, and very supportive of all I was going through. But my lack of self-esteem had held me back in high school, and I had missed the opportunity of a lifetime.

I had wanted to be like Grampy Miller, devoted and true to my wife all the days of my life. He had set such a great example for me, and I wanted to walk in his shoes. Partly because of this, I had been reluctant to leave Amanda when I had the opportunity. But I should have gone to my mother's house, when she first invited me, and gotten the psychiatric counseling that I needed. At that point in my life, I needed to focus on me and getting the help that was necessary.

Maybe things would have worked out between me and Amanda. The ironic piece is that I stayed to try to hold my marriage together, ignoring my own needs and not getting the help I needed. Yet, Amanda ended up divorcing me anyway. She didn't want to be married to someone who had a criminal history like mine, even though she had played a part in pushing me off the cliff.

When I was at the prison that allowed use of the library for study purposes, I had done a lot of research on the human brain. I enjoyed learning and increasing my knowledge, and I wanted to understand what had happened that day. Why had my brain and body not communicated and allowed me to make such a horrible mistake? What had happened just wasn't a part of my nature.

I discovered through my studies that while in the midst of a severe crisis, the brain can freeze and cease to function properly. It simply cannot handle the sensory overload. It takes time for the brain to do a little regrouping, kind of like a slow thawing process, before it can recover from a crisis and successfully move on.

That was my problem the day I shot Sierra McGovern. My brain was still in "freeze" mode. I was in the middle of the worst crisis I had ever faced. I had felt for quite some time that my world was falling apart, and it seemed as though it just had. Even though I knew it was coming, I hadn't made adequate plans regarding how to deal with it. So I found myself at a total loss. Where could I go? What would I do with my life now? How had my life become such a mixed up mess when I had promised myself it wouldn't? Did I really want to move in with my mother and burden her the way I had my wife? I had lots of questions with no answers, and it seemed there was no use for my life anymore.

All I had wanted to do that day was to kill myself and get the misery that had become my life over and done with. But Sierra McGovern had stepped in between me and my goal, which I had come very close to achieving. I have often reflected on why a woman would charge at a man with a loaded gun. Did she actually think she could come out the winner? If she had followed her boyfriend's example and retreated to the safety of their car, she could have survived the altercation, too. He had walked away physically uninjured, and she could have as well.

See, the thing is, I wasn't out looking for trouble that day. My life had fallen apart, but I wasn't ranting and raving about it, and seeking some form of vengeance. I wasn't looking for some innocent person to take my anger out on. True, I was definitely mad at life. Yet, with all I had been through, and as disappointed with life as I was, my intentions were only to take my frustrations out on myself. I wanted my life to be over. It had become too much for me to handle, and I just wanted out of it. I never, ever intended to end someone else's life instead.

Sometimes part of me wonders if it was some form of inner demon that took over, without my permission, and unleashed all my fury at life on this unsuspecting person. All the pent up anger of my physical discomforts, my failure of being unable to work and take care of my family, my anger at the beatings from Amanda, my complete frustration on how little control I had over my life. If that was the case, it would explain why I unloaded the full clip without realizing it. The angry demon kept firing the gun until there was nothing left to shoot.

The media labeled the events of that horrific day as "road rage." Maybe that was the case for Sierra, but I know that wasn't the case for me. No, it wasn't an evil demon, nor was it in reaction to all my frustrations from the failures and heartaches that I had faced in life. I know what motivated me that day. It was fear. It was a pure, saturating, unadulterated fear that caused me to react the way I did. My brain saw two men charging at me, looking like they were intent on performing bodily harm. I was scared to the core. I believe the fear factor and the need to protect myself kicked in. Self-preservation persisted, as ironically as that may sound. Wasn't I on the way to the ball field to kill myself? I guess I wanted my death to be at my own hand, and not the hands of a couple of strangers I had never met.

Also, as I think about the gun, to this day, I swear I was telling them to "Stop, stop, stop." Yet, what was happening in reality was that my gun was going "Pop, pop, pop." I slightly remember the blurred vision of a hand holding a gun, and seeing that gun flopping loosely around as it was being fired. For a split second in time, my brain thought it was a video game with an inexperienced shooter. But then as Sierra fell to the ground, the seriousness of what was happening became very real and slapped me right in the face. That apparition had been my hand, which was not inexperienced with guns. It just wasn't aware of what it was doing at the time.

It had really been the perfect storm, unfortunately. Everything had led up to this moment in time, and what I was going through had nothing to do with Sierra. She was just in the wrong place, at the wrong time, and chose to pick a fight with the wrong person. My brain had been paralyzed with fear, due to the current crisis. Unfortunately, my trigger finger had thawed out before my brain did.

I guess the bottom line is that I should not have been carrying a gun. I had known for quite sometime that my brain was not in the right place and that I needed professional help, yet I had chosen to carry a gun around with me. People bearing a heavy emotional load, complicated by a stressful way of life, should not be carrying guns. When a life is in as much of a chaotic state as mine was back then, nothing good can come from adding a gun to the mixture. I had started carrying a gun due to a fear of a convicted murderer moving into my neighborhood. Now, because of the gun I carried that day, I had become a convicted murderer myself.

True, I had intended to use the gun on myself. Never in my wildest dreams did I ever imagine I would have the ability to inflict harm such as this on another person. I had always avoided confrontation like the plague. I would sprint from it, if at all possible. And for the times when I couldn't flee because it came from Amanda, I tolerated it until it was over. I didn't grow aggressive and retaliate, or contemplate malicious ways to get even.

No, I should have brought the guns back to my dad's house and left them in his care. Without the gun, our confrontation on the side of that quiet road in the little town of Newton Falls would not have amounted to much. We might have called each other a few bad names. It might have possibly escalated to the point where we threw a punch or two. We might have had to call the police to resolve the issue. But if I hadn't had a gun, we would have all walked away and made it safely back home. Instead, Sierra's family had to learn to live without her, and I would spend the rest of my days wasting away in a cement cell, surrounded by evil people, with no hope for the future.

It was an incomprehensible thing that happened that day. Sierra McGovern had lost her life. Her daughter had lost her mother, and had to complete the rest of her childhood without her presence. Sierra's mother and siblings had to accept that their loved one was gone and never coming home again. It had been an incredibly shocking and painful experience for their family, one that you never really recover from. Having lost Little Shay, I knew what that pain felt like. I still thought of her frequently and missed her beautiful spirit. Life had not been the same without her.

However, what was even more unfathomable than their pain was the fact that I was the perpetrator. I was the one who had taken it all away from the McGovern family. Me — the one who was resilient, the one who had embraced life and determined that my life was going to be successful, full of meaning and purpose. And now I was a murderer. It was a title I would carry for the rest of my life. I could apologize until my final breath, but nothing could ever right the wrong that I had done. What was done was done, and there was no fixing the pain and suffering that I had caused in my moment of fear.

****

I often think back to the beginning of my trial on the very first day when they started jury selection. My mother and father were there, along with some of my aunts and my maternal grandfather. The court had called over a hundred people for jury duty, and they were sorting through them, one-by-one, to see which would fit the best. With all those who had responded to the call, along with the judge, the lawyers, the court officials, the reporters, and those from Sierra's family, the courtroom was packed full.

Sitting there looking around at all the different faces and the different age groups, I couldn't help but wonder where they had all come from and what their walk in life had been like. One prevailing thought kept coming to the surface, though - they were all there because of me. Whether they were there to support me, or whether they were there to seek justice against me, none of them would have been there that day if my life hadn't crossed paths with theirs.

That day made me realize that every life has an impact on the world. We can have a positive impact, or we can have a negative one. We can choose to do positive deeds all the days of our lives, making the world a better place, or we can let life get away from us and perform unthinkable acts of evil. People might remember you as a saint, or they might think you were the devil in the flesh. We all leave memories of the things we have done, whether they be for good or bad.

I had a few seconds of unforgivable and appalling decision making that took over my life and cast a dark shadow over the lives of others. It was a moment of time that I would give anything to erase. If I could remove one date from the pages of time, that would be the one. If history had only skipped that one fateful day, Sierra and I would still be an active part of life. She would have remained a vital part of her daughter's life and I, hopefully, could have gotten the help I needed.

Oh, how I long to remove that date from the pages of history, from the McGovern's painful memories of days gone by, and from the chronicles of Newton Falls record of yesteryears. If only it could be eradicated and simply forgotten for all time. But it is a part of my history now, as well as all those it affected, and forever recorded in the journal of our lives.

I frequently dream of Sierra, and often envy her until this day. She had died and gone to Heaven, where she could find rest and peace. I am still alive, but I am living in hell on earth. Could it be possible for hell to be much worse than what I face day after day, surrounded by evil, violence, and hatred? If only I could die, I would be at peace, too. Plus, I could apologize to her for what I had done to her and her family. But every morning, I wake up to the same ugly walls and face another day in hell.

Who knows why I am still alive. I guess only God Himself holds that answer. The reason I wake up every morning and fight to stay alive remains a mystery to me. Perhaps it is for my mother's sake. She has been so supportive ever since the day I pulled the trigger and my life fell apart. She worries constantly about me, and is good about keeping in touch. Maybe I am still alive for her. But even she can't right the wrong of what I did, as hard as she has tried.

No, anyone who thinks one moment of time is insignificant, needs to think again. Every minute is important. One moment in time can change the course of the rest of your life, as well as those around you. Sierra McGovern's life wasn't the only one that ended that night. Mine ended as well. Maybe not as profoundly and abruptly as hers, but that one thirty second segment of time in life robbed me of ever having any meaning or purpose for the rest of my days.

Throughout my years of incarceration, I have seen several of my fellow inmates pass away. Some have died from medical conditions. At times, these were complicated by the lack of medical care from prison administration. I truly believe if these prisoners had not been incarcerated, they would have survived their illness, as they could have received adequate medical care in the real world.

I recall one inmate who had appeared to be healthy and received a routine immunization as a precaution. The following day, I watched as he fell out of his chair and landed on the floor in a state of cardiac arrest. The prison staff attempted to resuscitate him, but they lacked the necessary skills and equipment to save him. He was returned to his family in a box.

And then there are the ones who took their own lives. Sometimes they hung themselves with their bed sheets. I have found that it doesn't take much for an every day item to become a weapon adequate enough to end a life. I would never have thought of my bed sheet as a weapon of destruction, but I have become very aware of how it could easily be used as one.

As I think back on those we have lost through the years, I think of them as the lucky ones. They have escaped the prison life, and no longer find themselves suffering in this hell on earth. This can't be described as living anyway. This is simply existing in a lost and forgotten world, despised and forsaken by society. Is there any point in continuing to exist this way, with no hope of ever getting out of here and having a life again?

One thing has become extremely clear to me. I cannot continue to live this way, day after day, for an entire forty-two year sentence. Maybe I will join those who have gone before me. In Heaven, I can rest with Grammy and Grampy Miller, and make amends with Sierra. I won't be afflicted with physical pain anymore. I won't have to watch my back constantly, fearing that an irate inmate might drive a homemade weapon into it. I won't have to eat food that's not fit for human consumption. I can simply float along with my beloved grandparents and finally be at peace.

So Grammy and Grampy Miller, get a cloud ready for me. I might just leave the pain of this world behind and come join you. We can relax and float along together on clouds of tranquility - just you and me, at peace together, drifting along and forever at rest. Don't be surprised if you soon find me knocking on those pearly gates, ready to make Heaven my home. Living in this hell on earth for forty-two years or floating on a cloud with Grammy and Grampy Miller – not much of a choice, is it? Keep your eyes open, my beloved grandparents. I might just head your way.

****

EPILOGUE

It is not my intention to let you know the ending of this story. I will admit that I love a happy ending. It is one of the reasons why I became a writer – to assure that my stories always finish on a happy note. However, as previously noted, this story is based on actual events, and real life doesn't always afford us the happy ending we dream about.

The conclusion of this story doesn't matter so much as what you have learned from it. I have always believed in the value of learning not just from our own mistakes, but also from the ones we witness around us. My hope is that this story has taught you that life is fragile. It is a gift that we need to cherish and honor, to use wisely and guard ourselves from tragic mistakes that might destroy more than just our own lives. What we do in life has a way of impacting all of those around us and society as a whole.

So if you believe in happy endings, as I do, then Jacob Miller didn't kill himself. His sentence was eventually reduced, he was released from prison, and he went on to impact society in a beneficial way. He was redeemed and didn't waste the rest of his days sitting in a barren, forsaken jail cell. Finally finding meaning and purpose for his life, he was able to complete his days on a positive note. That is my hope as well, so we will just believe it together.

Yet, as mentioned before, this story is based on a real life, an actual person. If truth be told, this is someone I have known for years, and can attest to his lack of criminal history prior to the shooting. His life is still on hold while we continue to wait for the justice system to work for us and allow him another chance at life. Perhaps it will, perhaps it will not. Only time will tell for sure.

However, let me leave you with these thoughts: Hold onto the concept that life is good, and precious, and worth giving it everything you've got. Walk carefully in life, and enjoy every minute of every day. Make good choices, and never let life get away from you. Appreciate every blessing you have, big or small. A bright, sunny day when you can wake up and do what you want for the day may seem insignificant, but it is one of the greatest blessings you will ever know. One never knows when everything can change, so take notice of the privileges of today. There is always something to be thankful for, even if it is nothing more than to be grateful that you have been blessed with another day of freedom.

Life is a gift. Use it wisely.

AN ENDING THOUGHT

"Every single time that I dream about that day, I try to fix it –
fix what went wrong. But, even while asleep –
I cannot fix it. I wake up in a cold sweat,
stare at the cement wall and begin to cry;
not just for myself,
but for everyone this tragedy has affected."

Anonymous

ACKNOWLEDGEMENTS

As with all the other books that I have written, I need to give credit where it is due. I have the ability to write the words and create the stories, but it takes more talent than what I possess to bring them into fruition. And for that, I must again give thanks to my family.

My usual crew was at work on this book as well. I thank my sister, Debra Cushman Femiak, for her artistic abilities in designing the book cover. Another sister, Linda Wright, provided the necessary proofreading skills, as well as always being available for counseling when I needed suggestions for chapter titles or ideas that kept me perplexed.

My niece, Michelle Wright, once again worked her magic on the computer. Her skills with formatting (and using programs I didn't even know exist) prepared the manuscript for submission for publication. I thank her for the many hours it took to get things just right.

Also, with the nature of this book, I must acknowledge my friend, whose story this is based on. His actions or, actually, one-time unfortunate reaction, truly showed us all how fragile life can be. My hope and prayer is that God's good graces will be with him and help him to be able to redeem some portion of his life.

And special thanks to you, the reader, for following through to the conclusion of this story. I hope this book meets its intended goal of aiding others in making good choices in life, thus resulting in a positive lifestyle and avoiding the confinements of prison. All of us can make a beneficial impact on society in some way. It doesn't necessarily need to be a major feat. Simple acts of kindness done for those we meet along the way can help to make the world a better place for everyone. And always remember – good choices equal a good life.

OTHER BOOKS BY THE AUTHOR

Everybody has a bad day sometimes, but Mary Davis is having twelve of them – in a row! With a husband named Joseph, this couple knew Christmas would always be special to them. But packing twelve adult children and their families into one day of holiday fun proves to be less than joyful.

So Mary has come up with the perfect plan. She will invite each child to come home, one day at a time, thus stretching out the holiday season and avoiding the chaos of a houseful of not-so-holiday cheer. With a plan like that, what could possibly go wrong?

But day after day of her holiday plan leaves Mary scrambling to try to save the day. With a resilient attitude (and the support of her faithful husband) she somehow manages to survive all twelve days.

A Twelve Davis Christmas *is a comical view of a mother's love for her children, her efforts to give them her best, with a blend of Murphy's Law folded in. If anything can go wrong, it will happen to Mary and Joseph Davis – and their tribe of twelve.*

OTHER BOOKS BY THE AUTHOR

Abigail Carter would not deny that she had been blessed with three beautiful children. As a mother, her love for her children was as genuine as it comes. However, it seemed that recently someone had stolen her eldest daughter, Joy, and replaced her with a teenage nightmare. Then when her son, Corey, crashes his ATV into her brand new car and her youngest daughter, Holly, falls out of the tree and breaks her arm, Abigail knows she needs help. Keeping this family safe is beyond her human means.

Her husband, Russell, does all he can to help provide harmony in the family, but it just doesn't seem to be enough. Something has to be done for the safety of her children, and to maintain her sanity. So Abigail goes to the highest power she knows – right to the throne room of God.

At her request, God sends three angels to help out. But will these rusty humans have what it takes to keep them safe? At times, it seems like the heavenly trio has met their match with the three Carter children.

***Angels for Abigail** is a fun, fictional story of family trials and the heavenly visitors who are doing their best to try to keep the Carter children on track, safe from themselves, and out of trouble. But which trio will be the victors – the angels, or the kids they were sent to protect?*

OTHER BOOKS BY THE AUTHOR

Kitty Litter: Thoughts from the Heart *is a sprinkling of uplifting thoughts, designed to give life a fresh, new aroma and help the reader see past the unpleasant aspects of life. It is comprised of three sections:*

- *The Art of Living*
- *The Joys of Parenting*
- *For the Spirit.*

Some thoughts are geared toward encouraging overwhelmed parents. Others are basic thoughts on the components of life itself and things that cross our paths simply as a side effect of being human. Some articles take on a spiritual tone and address the deeper meanings in life.

Wherever you may be on your walk in life, ***Kitty Litter: Thoughts from the Heart*** *has a message for you. Don't give up on this thing called life. It has too much to offer to waste time hanging out in the litter box.*

Let ***Kitty Litter*** *help you muster up some courage, put a smile back on your face, and find the strength to step out of the litter box to give life another chance.*

CHILDREN'S BOOKS BY THE AUTHOR

After the Snowflakes is a fully illustrated children's book about winter time activities. Each beautifully illustrated page shows a different event that celebrates fun things we can do after the snowflakes fall, including a few pages showing how different snowflakes could look. It ends with a playful poem about the uniqueness of snowflakes, encouraging the reader to get outside and enjoy the winter.

Sunny Boy is an illustrated children's book that discusses the role of the sun from an animated perpective. He starts to feel rejected when people don't appreciate him, but comes to realize the importance of the role he plays in the world around him. It is also a story of relationships and working together, as he forms a true friendship with Whispi the Cloud.